MY FIVE NIGHT
Fling

Maci Dillon

My Five Night Fling
British Billionaires Book One

Maci Dillon

This book is a work of fiction. Any references to real events, real people, and real places are used fictitiously. Other names, characters, places, and incidents are products of the author's imagination, and any resemblance to persons, living or dead, actual events, organizations, or places is entirely coincidental.

All rights are reserved. This book is intended for the purchaser of this e-book ONLY. No part of this book may be reproduced or transmitted in any form or by any means, graphic, electronic, or mechanical, including photocopying, recording, taping, or by any information storage retrieval system, without the express written permission of the author. All songs, song titles, and lyrics contained in this book are the property of the respective songwriters and copyright holders.

Disclaimer: The material in this book contains graphic language and sexual content and is intended for mature audiences ages 18 and older.

All efforts have been made to ensure the use of correct grammar and punctuation in the book. If you find any errors, please email Maci Dillon at admin@macidillonauthor.com
Thank you.

ISBN: 979-8451578087

Editing by Swish Design & Editing
Proofreading by Swish Design & Editing
Book Design by Swish Design & Editing
Cover Design by Opium House Creatives
Cover Image Copyright 2021
First Edition 2021
Copyright © 2021 Maci Dillon
All Rights Reserved

DEDICATIN

*For all the career-focused women who want their
happily ever after too.
Anything is possible when we open our
hearts to possibility*

GLOSSARY

This series is set in London, UK and written in American English. You will find some British slang used in dialogue which you may not have heard before, so I have listed a few below.

Black Pudding - cooked pork or beef blood
Blimey - used to express surprise at something
Bonkers - mad, crazy
Cock-up - mistake, failure
Digs - housing, home
Dog's Bollocks - admirable, good at something
Gobby - used to describe someone who talks a lot
Haggis - minced sheep's heart, liver, lungs
Jiffy - to do something immediately
Knackered - extremely tired, exhausted
Plastered - drunk, intoxicated
Plonker - foolish person
Scotch Egg - boiled egg wrapped in sausage meat,

coated with breadcrumbs and baked
Scrummy Nosh - delicious food
Shambles - mess, confusion
Spotted Dick - baked pudding, dessert with dried fruit
Taking the mickey - to tease or make jokes
Tanked - drunk, intoxicated
Toad in the Hole - sausages cooked in Yorkshire pudding batter

MY FIVE NIGHT
Fling

Chapter 1

KASSIDY

What the hell?

Debris floats from the sky and lands on my face.

For protection, I pull my sunglasses over my eyes and swipe my hand over my face as another light drop of heavenly residue tickles my nose.

Three steps outside London Central Station, I'm sandwiched between businessmen on their phones and families with young children rushing to keep in step with each other.

Having no clue what direction I should be walking, I push ahead with the flow of foot traffic and hope for the best.

Shaking my head, I brush off the shit falling all around me. Snow-white satin feathers whisp across my face and land on my sunglasses, obscuring my view.

Then it hits me.
No fucking way.
Squinting, I remove my glasses and move my face to look at the sky.
It's snowing.
Waves of excitement build as I anticipate a snowy holiday. At first, it was so light, the flakes had disappeared before they landed on the ground, but the further I walk, the heavier the snowflakes fall, creating a thin icy blanket beneath my feet.

My grin expands the width of my face until my cheeks ache from the intrusion. My nose is frozen solid, so I pull my beanie further over my ears to protect them from the icy breeze.

Snowfalls in late March aren't the norm, but crazier things have been known to happen. With spring settling in, I had hoped and prayed to see snow for the first time, though I wasn't optimistic. With all my heart, I prayed to the weather gods on my flight over, and here I am, walking among the magic of my childhood dreams. Ever since I took this assignment and booked a stopover in London on my return home, I dreamed of a snowy visit to the Big Smoke.

As a little girl, sitting on the rickety front porch of my parents' old Queenslander in the scorching hot Australian summers, I had waited for this moment. Or rather, I imagined myself dancing the night away under the streetlight, snow falling all around me. With my prince, of course.

Excuse me, no judgment.

I was young, innocent, and believed in fairy tales. Hell, I still do.

Thirty years later, my design and marketing degree has landed me a dream position with an international company, affording me a jet-setter's lifestyle.

I bounce from client to client, contract to contract, around the globe, living the single woman's dream—the world at my feet, men too, all served up with a no-strings-attached expectation.

With my career, I thrive on learning from the best gurus worldwide to catapult my success. Climbing the ranks in a male-dominated field isn't easy, but sure as this snow falling on my face, it is possible.

I'm goal-driven and motivated by success. My friends love my dedication and enthusiasm, even though they often tease me about my need for power. It's one hundred percent true, I can't dispute that fact.

One thing I promised myself on this journey was never to lose sight of myself. To stay true to me, never stray from the unexpected, the fun. My wild side.

Okay, it's not that wild. But still.

Shh, okay, you got me. I enjoy life on the wild side.

Even strong career-orientated women need an outlet. A way to unwind, an excuse to let go and enjoy the beauty life has to offer. Believe me, I'm no stranger to letting my hair down, but I can count the moments on one hand where I did something spontaneous over the past few years.

London is my fresh canvas. A chance to redefine me, shop for unnecessary items, drink strange beers, and eat lots of weird shit.

London.
Five nights.
A fairy tale imagining.
The perfect backdrop.

Caught up in the fantasy of my trip, I disregard the onlookers and pedestrians sharing the pathway. Right where I stand, I throw my arms out wide, my head falls backward, and I twirl like the ballerina I'll never be.

"Shit, sorry!" I gasp, clasping my hands over my mouth as I open my eyes to find a mother and her child in front of me. Both of them are wearing comical expressions despite me accidentally swiping them with my flailing arms.

"My apologies, I guess I lost track of where I was." I'm caught up in the moment.

The woman laughs and points to my backpack strapped tightly over my shoulders. "First time in

London or first-time experiencing snow?"

My lips pull into a dreamy grin.

"Both." On my visit to Prague for the business part of my trip, I saw snow on the hills in the distance, but there was no snowfall while I was there.

The woman, still holding the young boy's hand, offers a smile in return. "Enjoy your stay."

"Thank you. I have no doubt I will." A chuckle escapes me as I fall back into the fantasy world of finding my one true love.

If only my grandmother were still with us.

Poor Grandma, she listened to me babble on about dreams as a child for countless hours on our family porch. After all these years, she'll be thrilled to learn I'm still the same little girl inside.

As I poorly navigate my way through the streets of Central London, I feel her presence by my side.

Two-story buses loaded with tourists pointing and taking photos buzz by me. The guides are talking into a microphone and sharing their local knowledge.

Yeah, I'm over the top, far too swept up in the fantasy of this trip, but fuck it, I deserve this. After a week conference in Prague, the days so long I barely glimpsed the streets in daylight hours, this brief five-night stopover is exactly what I need.

No work talk.

Goals, what goals?

Chasing success is for women *not* on vacation.

Five nights—all about me and me alone.

For two years now, colleagues, friends, and family have continued to harass me about taking a break.

'Enjoy being a single woman in your mid-twenties,' they would say. 'Live your best life before you settle down and have children of your own.'

The unwelcome advice was relentless, yet here I am.

This is me, breaking free—freedom from long hours at the office and sleepless nights. The only sleepless nights I'm interested in this week will be filled with dirty sex—one-night hookups and no strings.

As much as my heart sings with my love of fairy tale endings, I have no time or patience for romance in my life. I have worked too damn hard to press pause on my career for any emotional relationship.

Married to my work. That's me.

The sexual kind of relationships, though? A whole different bag of balls.

London is my playground, and hell, I'm going to make it my bitch.

I cringe any time I flashback to my last intimate relationship—the kind with emotions involved. Midway through college, it proved nothing but a distraction. Nothing good was ever going to come from it. I hated to admit it, but I lowered my standards more often than I cared to admit back then. The sex drew me in, and I stayed in a place I knew, one that felt comfortable. There was no excitement, no challenge, no experience. Even the sex became boring after a while, and in the end, both of us would walk away feeling less than satisfied and less like ourselves. What was the point?

Miniature cars with incessant horns beep around me as I thoughtlessly step into the street. I jump backward, almost toppling over with the weight of my backpack, straps digging harshly into my shoulders. Once I safely make it across the street, I take a seat on the park bench to gain my bearings.

My stomach rumbles, proof the airline breakfast of fake bacon and powdered eggs were exactly as I thought—utter rubbish and a waste of energy trying to chew and process it.

Okay, I'm getting hungry now, bordering on the edge of *hangry.* Never a good place to be.

Releasing my bag to relieve my back, I pull out the oversized map I grabbed at the airport. Yes, I know. It would be easier to punch the destination into maps on my phone, but where's the fun in that?

I need to figure out where I am versus where I need to go. Snowflakes fall heavier and faster around me as I unfold the map the best I can while wearing gloves.

I glance up at the sky, undeniably darker now than when I first arrived. Quickly, I tuck the map away and attach myself to my backpack, securing it around my middle.

Time to get moving, find a warm place to pull up a chair, and eat my weight in tasty food.

The increasing moisture in the air and icy coverage on the rough, uneven footpaths have me concentrating on my steps more than usual. Now isn't the time to show off my lack of balance. Thankfully, I chose street-worthy long boots with a low heel for the flight over.

Cautiously, I weave through the growing crowd of pedestrians, searching for a familiar street name, shop, or park from the research I had done before my arrival. From the moment a lonely snowflake landed on my nose, I continue to walk in the direction my feet carry me, marveling at the beauty of my surroundings.

A deep grumble in the pit of my stomach urges me to move a little faster and a little smarter, so I continue along the street I'm on. The worst-case scenario, I'm down with flagging a cab to deliver me to my hotel, which I know is surrounded by restaurants, cafés, and pubs. Finding a meal will be a simple feat then.

A rowdy group of men ahead capture my attention as they scurry across the road and stumble through a heavy wooden door. I follow, and as I approach the entrance, I swiftly turn from the footpath without a moment's consideration as to what I'm walking into.

As I push open the door, warmth invades my ice-cold cheeks, and my nose tingles as it begins to defrost. My stomach somersaults in response to the delicious aroma of food that fills the air.

I remove my gloves, rub my hands together, and enjoy the warmth from the friction as I glance around the café. A wood fire burns in the center of the room, giving off a soft intimate glow. A quick assessment of the diners suggests it's a popular place for couples to meet over lunch, share a kiss and the events of the day. Girlfriends gather over coffee and croissants, sharing laughs and their dirty secrets.

Jealousy punches me in the ribs as a familiar feeling of homesickness trickles through me. I miss home, and it's going on ten days since I clocked up some serious girl time. While social media makes it easy to keep in contact, it isn't the same.

I make a mental note to Skype Miah, Raven, and Chloe when I make it to my room. As I search the café for a free table, I consider sending my mother a quick message to let her know I arrived safely. While my mother and I aren't particularly close, we do stay in contact, especially when traveling. A simple photo or occasional text is often enough.

First, I desperately need to find a seat to relieve

my aching muscles.

Focus, Kassidy.

Suddenly, a cold draft hits full force from behind me. Quickly, I'm knocked off balance, and I'm seconds away from landing face-first into a row of memorabilia lining the walls.

Chapter 2

KASSIDY

"Blimey," a frustrated male voice permeates my ears.

Diners gasp, a notable change to the laughter which filled the room only moments ago. A strong hand wraps over my right shoulder, and an iron forearm braces my midsection pulling me upright, only milliseconds from cracking my head open on the display cabinet.

Grateful for being saved from a gash on the head and further unwanted attention, I'm torn between showing my gratitude and wishing the floor would open wide and swallow me whole.

Horrified I had caused a scene, my body shakes uncontrollably. More so due to the embarrassment of the situation than the shock or the cold.

Or is it the result of being trapped inside the

arms of a stranger?

"Fuck, are you okay? Why the hell were you standing in the..." his voice trails off as I turn to face him.

My assailant and savior.

Deep brown eyes stare down at me with empathy and something else.

Heat.

Any trace of anger or frustration he first had is long gone.

"I... I'm sorry. So sorry." Words fail me as humiliation sets in. Not only are the most gorgeous chocolate eyes tracing the length of my body, but his entourage of onlookers observe me with a mixture of amusement and pity.

"Trust J to cock-up a first impression," one of his female friends scoff, her glare burning holes in my thick skin.

I blame lack of sleep, hunger, and mortification for the swell of tears building in my eyes. I act quickly to subdue them, squeezing the bridge of my nose between my forefingers as I glance at the door.

I can do this.

In seconds, I could be on the other side of that door. I should dash out of here as if nothing happened. Unfortunately, my legs are jelly and refuse to follow my mind's lead. As if sensing the pique of my emotional crisis, the hot guy with his eyes on me curses his group of friends and directs them to a table in the far corner.

Each of them, the guy and the two women he's with, respond to his instruction without question. He is the ringleader of their group. Oddly, he appears to be more like the black sheep, dressed casually in shabby dark denim jeans and bomber jacket as opposed to the business suits and professional attire worn by the others.

"Roman," he calls to the good-looking, dark-haired man behind the counter who's completely oblivious to our awkward situation. He raises his eyes briefly and nods to the guy in front of me as he serves a customer at the register. "Mind if my friend here stores her bag in your office while she eats?"

Wait, what? "Oh no, it's not, umm—"

What's his name?

"Sure, man, go ahead," he yells, continuing to serve the customers while also ordering the staff around.

I remove my beanie and check my head—I must have a concussion.

Nope.

I'm confused and slightly delirious all on my own. Plus, I'm still standing in the same place I was knocked off-center only a few moments ago.

I'm a fucking accident waiting to happen.

"My bag is fine, honestly. I'm leaving now," I tell him, pointing at the door. A quick glimpse of the snowstorm through the windows has me regretting the words as quickly as they leave my mouth.

The stranger, the sexy-as-fuck dark-haired stranger who has me scrambling for words, eyes me curiously. An I-don't-believe-you-for-a-second expression spreads across his face.

Then he smirks.

Gah! One of those lopsided playful grins. The kind which makes single women like me giddy on the inside. "Sure, you are, sweetheart. You Australian?"

I nod feebly.

His smirk extends into a full-blown smile and, fuck!

I'm mush. Where am I?

"Here's the thing. I nearly knocked you ass over tit. The least I should offer you is lunch."

The least he should offer.

Hmm, what's the most he'll offer?

Wasting no time waiting on my response, he boldly slides the straps of my backpack from my shoulders. This guy is completely unafraid to be in my personal space. *Is it weird that I'm onboard with this?*

Goosebumps inundate my body as his fingertips brush my hands.

"Please accept. It's my way of apologizing for the shambles." He grins, throwing my bag over his shoulder. "Besides, denying my right to buy a beautiful woman lunch would be considered rude."

I breathe through the urge to roll my eyes at him and smirk instead.

He nods at the menu on the wall. "Select what you want to feast on, and I'll be out to take your order in a jiffy."

I watch as he disappears with everything I own apart from my handbag. I use these few moments to gather myself and glance toward the corner of the café where, whatever his name is, banished his friends. They were happily engaged in conversation as if they never arrived with one extra.

I selfishly hope we don't join the group. Exhaustion sweeps through my veins rapidly, and small talk with one stranger sounds like enough of a challenge for me today.

When the guy flippantly returns to my side, my curiosity peaks. "What if I've already eaten?"

He glances sideways at me. "You haven't."

His answer is sharp and short as he moves to the front of the line and orders for both of us. I'm too tired to care what he orders and allow him to remove my jacket and direct us to the bench seat adjoining the window.

My senses awaken as his palm settles over my lower back as he guides me to a table away from the crowd, his friends, and prying eyes. Not to mention the view of the snow-covered street through the window, and we're close to the fireplace.

It's perfect.

We climb across the bench seat, sitting side by side rather than across from each other. This way, we both have a street view and avoid awkward eye contact, and it will be easier when the conversation between strangers becomes dull or non-existent. There's every chance we have nothing at all in common.

I instantly wish I had taken a few minutes to freshen up before leaving the subway. At this point, I can only hope I appear more put together and smell fresher than I am.

A young waiter arrives with a bottle of sauvignon blanc. I'm both pleased and slightly concerned. A cocktail of exhaustion, wailing emotions, and alcohol spells a recipe for disaster.

Now isn't the time to be reckless.

All alone in a strange city.

Lunch and wine with a sexy-as-sin stranger.

Ugh, what could go wrong?

I'm ninety-nine percent certain I couldn't say no to this guy when sober, let alone after a few glasses of nice wine.

Yes, it's exactly what I want my days and nights to be filled with, but not in this order. First, I require a hot bath and sleep. I vow to sip my wine conservatively, at least to start with.

"I spotted you on the street, you know. You appeared to be intrigued by the snow. And dare I say, a little lost and disgruntled." My head whips around in his direction, my mouth open, ready to set him straight. But he continues, not missing a beat, "You walked in here moments before we did."

My gaze follows him as he fills our glasses.

"Quite intuitive, aren't you?" I challenge. "It's a shame you didn't wait a little longer before following me in here. The *shambles* as you put it might have been avoided altogether." I grin over the top of my glass.

He laughs. It's a beautiful sound as if his accent doesn't have me all kinds of twisted already. Those dimples and perfect teeth add to the package. And his Adam's apple. I'm afraid my body will start to purr out loud if I continue to eyeball him.

"Funny. I assumed you stopped in here when you saw us heading this way." He scoffs playfully.

My head falls back with an easy chuckle. "How conceited of you," I tease.

Still smiling, he continues, "Café Zest is our usual meeting place for lunch with friends and colleagues." He points over his shoulder at the table of three. "Normally, there's a larger group of us, but a snowstorm on the outskirts of town last night kept a few people from making it into the city this morning."

I admit I find it odd he's happy to dine with a stranger instead of his group, especially if this is their weekday thing. But who am I to argue?

"So, you're visiting from Australia. For how long?" he asks.

I raise my eyebrows in question. "What makes you think I'm not staying here indefinitely?"

His head cocks to one side, his brows pull together, and his delicious lips twitch as he contemplates the question. "I'll go with the limited luggage you arrived with."

"So, you're not psychic?"

It's his turn to be miffed by my question.

"Psychic, wow. I've been called many things in my lifetime but never psychic."

"Okay, let's digress. First, you stage a knockout as you enter the café, knowing I was standing in that exact spot. Second, you realize I'm five seconds from falling apart, so you offer to buy me lunch, which I may have already eaten, but you're certain I have not, and you know exactly what I want to eat, so you order for me."

He chuckles, and we enjoy a sip of our wine. "I'm chuffed," he goads me. "Am I the dog's bollocks or what?"

I burst out laughing, "Dog's bollocks... what... why? Please explain."

Our laughter fills the café. Between him and I, we're a comical mess. Out of the corner of my eye, I see his friends across the café are amused by our antics too. Well, two of them, anyway.

On a quieter note, he explains, "It's like saying

how *awesome* am I. British slang, you'll get the gist of it during your stay." It's refreshing chilling out with a stranger who has entertainment value. As I finish off my glass, I circle back to the question he first asked. "I'm on my way home following a work conference in Prague. Five work-free nights in London is my treat to myself."

"Five nights, huh?" He taps his fingers on his thigh. "I guess I'll need to work quickly."

Chapter 3

KASSIDY

"Work quickly for what?"

Ugh, enough with the grin.

His mouth is impeccable.

His lips, so kissable.

I ignore the reason behind the comment and his grin to visit the restroom before our meal arrives. Hopefully, a trip to the ladies' room will subdue the tingly sensations accompanying the second glass of wine.

Entering the bathroom, I catch a glimpse of my ghastly reflection in the mirror.

"Kill me, now," I groan.

Sleep eluded me during the flight, and after a busy night prior, my lack of rest has resulted in dark circles under my bloodshot eyes.

I'm the queen of hot messes today. *Go me*, I

encourage myself.

After relieving myself, I splash water on my face and dig through my small handbag for some powder, mascara, and gloss. I apply sparingly to avoid the dark-haired stranger assuming I'm making myself more visually pleasing for him.

I roll on a little perfume beneath my ears, do a quick spot check of myself in the mirror, and walk out. There's only so much a girl can do with limited supplies. I come to an abrupt halt just outside the door when met with a snarky-looking chick filled to the brim with attitude.

What the fuck?

"Whoever you think you are and whatever you're trying to get from Jarett, it's not going to happen. I suggest you move on already." The brunette spits her words at me, her fingers doing way too much talking for my liking.

I open my mouth to tell her exactly what she can do with her unsolicited advice when she continues, "Jarett might fit the bill for a random hookup, but you..." she snarls, pointing her finger close to my chest, "... aren't his type. And he's *way* out of your league."

Pushing her finger out of my space, I step away from her. I don't care who this bitch thinks she is, but I do recognize her as the one who arrived with the group and death-stared at me after my run-in with *Jarett*.

At least now he has a name.

This bitch turns her nose up as her eyes wander over my body from head to toe, stopping at my breasts. I stand still, feeling cheap and exposed.

For a fleeting second, that is.

"He prefers his women a little less curvy with a chest bigger than his own." She snickers bitterly.

My fists clench tightly. Words lodge in my throat for three-point five nanoseconds as I stare at this unbelievable mammal. *The nerve of it!*

Honestly, I want to be the better woman and walk away as if she weren't here. I try to swallow my pride and keep my thoughts to myself. My grandma's words come back to me. *There's no such thing as try. You either do, or you don't.*

I don't.

Today, I can't.

This bitch has gotten under my skin on the wrong motherfucking day.

"Sweetie, bitterness and rejection don't look good on you. I doubt you have a clue what Jarett wants, but it will never be *you.* He doesn't strike me as the type to chase after childish skanks. But good luck." I don't wait for a response. Instead, gloating internally as her mouth falls open, and her eyes widen at the insult, but she has nothing.

A typical sociopath.

As the food is arriving, I make it back to our table.

Anxiety spreads like wildfire through my body. Heat flushes my cheeks as I gulp my wine, and my heart pounds with guilt.

The wench deserved it, but I'm not a girl who lets things get to me. It's not my style to lash out at others. And what would this hot guy, Jarett, think of me for insulting one of his friends?

"Roman, this is—" his voice breaks off, and he eyes me inquisitively, prompting me silently for a name. I hesitate a little, strangely turned on at the fact he had not yet asked for it.

I turn and offer my hand. "Hello, Roman, I'm Kassidy. Lovely to meet you." I offer my sweetest of smiles.

Roman raises my hand to his mouth, planting a chaste kiss on the back. Out of the corner of my eye, I spot Jarett rolling his eyes with a shake of his head.

"Yes, meet my brother, Roman. He owns this place," Jarett adds with a sweep of his hands, clearly proud of his brother's achievements.

My eyebrows raise a little in response to learning these two gorgeous men are brothers. Roman is obviously older, though equally as charming and handsome.

"Nice place you have here," I tell him, my eyes darting around at the artwork on the walls for the first time. My stomach rumbles so loudly I'm thankful for the laughter which erupts at the table behind us. At this point, I'm terrified I'll start foaming at the mouth if I can't get my lips around the ravioli in front of me.

It's screaming my name.

"Thank you," Roman smiles. Please forgive my little bro. His tact is lacking." He jabs his brother in the side as he speaks.

"What! Why would you say that?" Jarett whines, faking insult.

"The little I know about women, I guess I always assumed asking their name before inviting them to enjoy lunch and a bottle of fine wine was a prerequisite."

I can't help but laugh at their banter. Roman isn't wrong, but I'm not bothered by it one bit.

What I'd love to confirm is whether this is Jarett's normal route to seduction. I imagine it rarely fails him. Unquestionably a ladies' man, I envision him wining and dining random women, fucking them stupid, and moving on before the sun rises.

I clench my thighs together and lift a silent prayer before I return my focus to Roman. "Thank you for allowing me to store my things in your office. And for this food, it smells divine." I stir the rich tomato-based sauce through the pockets of pasta, salivating at the aromatic steam wafting from the bowl.

Taking the subtle hint my food is calling, Roman answers, "Anytime. I hope London is kind to you. Be sure to drop in again before you leave."

"I'll be sure to."

And I will.

If I don't die of starvation in the meantime.

"Enjoy your lunch and stay out of the blizzards." Roman flashes a rich grin, like his brother's, and leaves us to enjoy our meal. I have many questions for Jarett, but first, I seek salvation from my hunger pains.

We eat in comfortable silence. I daydream peacefully as the snow falls against the window, consciously aware of Jarett's eyes on me. My body responds to his perusal in ways I'd like to explore further.

Any other day.

When his friends stop by our table on their way out, I'm curious whether they all work together or meet on their lunch breaks from various nearby offices.

Jarett is quick to introduce the women. "Sophia, this is Kassidy." He points to the more gorgeous of the two—a tall, fit woman in her late thirties, I'm guessing. "Kassidy is visiting from Australia." I offer her my hand. "Sophia is my sister."

Oddly, it felt good to hear him say *sister*.

We exchange pleasantries, and I learn Sophia is the sister between Jarett and Roman.

"And this is Claire." He points to the nasty woman I met on my visit to the restroom. He offers no other introduction. I simply nod and offer an incredibly weak smile.

The guy with them thrusts his hand out and introduces himself. "I need no introduction, I'm more than capable of speaking for myself in the presence of a beautiful woman," he drools.

I shake his hand. "And you are?"

Everyone except Claire laughs.

"Right, I'm Damon. Jarett's wingman. God knows he needs it."

Jarett rolls his eyes. "Apologies in advance... Damon can be a bit gobby sometimes."

Damon throws Jarett a deadpan look before he turns toward the door to leave.

"Nice to meet you," I yell after them as Damon and Claire exit the café.

Sophia hovers a moment longer. "Kassidy, I apologize for Claire's behavior earlier."

Inwardly, I cringe, and my eyes dart to Jarett. "I overheard her as I was coming out of Roman's office. I was going to step in, but there was no need. You had it under control." She laughs sweetly.

"Claire has been chasing after Jarett since high school, and she's pissed at any other women he notices or has time for."

She pats my forearm in a friendly gesture. I have a feeling she has endured the wraith of Claire personally a time or two or witnessed her bullshit enough to pity those in her line of fire.

Jarett's confused expression morphs into bewilderment as he digests what Sophia is referring to. Annoyed by Claire's obsession, he apologizes profusely after Sophia fills him in. I sink lower in my chair, wanting to hide in the remains of my ravioli.

I don't need people to step in or come to my rescue.

"I've never shown her the slightest bit of interest," he spits out, more to Sophia than me. I need no explanation. "I wish she'd get over this ridiculous obsession and move on. It's embarrassing, not to mention infuriating."

Frustration rolls off Jarett in waves, and I'd recognize his inherent dislike of Claire from a mile away. I wonder about their connection to her if neither of them enjoys her company, yet she joins them for lunch.

When Jarett grazes my hand and squeezes it, I'm momentarily unnerved by the gesture. Sophia's eyes follow the exchange, and a ghost of a grin touches her lips.

"I must be going, but Kassidy?" Sophia puts on her coat as she addresses me. "We're having drinks tonight at Maximum, a friend's speakeasy not far from here. Why don't you join us? Killer cocktails, live music, and dancing. It's always fun."

Honestly, I doubt any time spent with Sophia could be anything less than fun. She carries a certain presence about her, one I admire and it intrigues me.

She's bold and beautiful. Loud and charismatic. It isn't hard to imagine her as the center of attention everywhere she goes. Her charm is a deeply engrained character trait in this family tree.

Charm is a winner in my book.

I speak their language.

I take pride in my appearance and dress to impress. I carry myself with vigor, understand my strengths, and ooze confidence but in a humble way. I'm not beautiful like Sophia, but I hold the attention of men wherever I go.

Average height, symmetrical curves, and toned in the right areas, the gym is good to me, but I'm not a girl who lives for the gym. I'm a foodie and love eating my way through different cities. Plus, I do love a drink or ten.

Before I have a chance to answer, Jarett confirms for the both of us. I don't have it in me to object, nor call him out for answering for me once again.

"Fantastic, can't wait!" She grins and leans in to deliver a peck on my cheek. "See you tonight."

Plans for my first night. *Check.*

A young waiter arrives to clear the dishes from the table once we're done. Jarett leans in and whispers in my ear while my skin ignites, and every inch sparks with excitement at his proximity, "Join me for dinner before drinks. I want you to myself a little longer."

I can't deny our chemistry. It vibrates down to my bones.

Having enjoyed an hour together over nice food and a bottle of wine, I learned many things about this stranger who accosted me. The more I learn, the more I want to discover. Each new piece of information draws me in deeper.

"Sounds perfect," I agree.

Jarett excuses himself to retrieve my belongings while I polish off the last of my wine.

When he returns wearing my backpack, I frown at him. "I should head off and find where I'm staying," I explain, extending my hand to retrieve my things. "If you want a coherent date tonight, I'll need to at least have a few hours of beauty sleep."

Not willing to hand over my luggage, my gaze travels up his body.

If *seduction* has a face, it's staring at me right now. A warm glimmer in those brown eyes sends a shiver down my spine.

"Oh, believe me, sweetheart..." he leans in and whispers in my ear, "... I want you to be fully coherent tonight."

I swallow.

Hard.

Chapter 4

KASSIDY

Together, we walk out of Café Zest in search of my home for the next five nights. Jarett insists on walking with me, committed to my safe arrival. Honestly, I'm grateful for the company, but my body aches, and I'm deteriorating quickly. Plus, Jarett needs my location for when he picks me up tonight, I guess.

It turns out I'm staying at the Central Inn, midway between Roman's café and Jarett's art gallery. Yeah, he owns a gallery and specializes in buying and selling work by local and international artists.

We walk into the hotel's reception area, and the young woman behind the desk drools at the sight of Jarett. I give her my name and offer my card for payment, and still, she doesn't acknowledge me.

Am I fucking invisible?

"Miss, my girlfriend here wants to check-in, please," Jarett announces, a hint of irritation in his tone. I snap my head toward him, and he winks, taking my hand.

The woman shakes free of her trance and gets on with her job. "Of course, Mr. Evans. Right away."

Mr. Evans? They know each other.

I check-in, and we step into the elevator.

"Dare I ask what that was about?"

Jarett shakes his head and sighs deeply. "People read too much."

His response confuses the shit out of me.

"She practically drooled over you and called you Mr. Evans, like you're royalty or something." I chuckle nervously. "Oh my God, tell me you're not royalty."

Jarett frowns at me a moment before he opens his mouth to speak. Then he stops and says, "No, not royalty."

I breathe a sigh of relief.

We make it to my room, and I take my bag from Jarett without inviting him in. I thank him for his hospitality, and he pulls me forward, planting a kiss.

Not a peck-on-the-cheek-between-friends type of kiss.

No, he teases me with his soft lips on mine and leaves me wanting more.

"Pick you up at seven."

I nod and promptly shut the door in his face.

Trust me, it sounds worse than it is.

I hope he doesn't find it rude after he's been so adorably sweet. The truth is the wall I've been on the verge of crashing into for the past hour has come plummeting down.

After a fulfilling lunch and a bottle of wine, a hot shower is calling my name.

JARETT

I stand in the empty corridor staring at the door to Kassidy's room—the door she promptly closed in my face—and I grin. The woman has class, and she's sassy too.

I like her.

Pulling out my phone, I do a quick Google search for Jarett Evans. When nothing new comes up, I pray it never does.

Happy with the turn of events for the day following a bad business meeting at the gallery this morning, I elect to take a casual walk to my office.

I'm not going to lie, I am pretty chuffed.

My feet walk in the general direction of the gallery while my head is stuck in the metaphorical clouds. The corners of my mouth pull upward of their own accord.

When was the last time I smiled like this?

Even the moody weather can't ruin my afternoon. I wander mindlessly through the streets completely oblivious to my surroundings until my phone vibrates in my pocket.

Sophia's smiling face lights up the display when I pull it from my jacket.

"Little sister, what must I do for you?" I answer, knowing full well she's chasing details on the blonde bombshell I shared lunch with.

"Little brother, you dirty manwhore," she jokes. "Kassidy is adorable. Are you sure you two only met today at the café?"

"Yes, Soph," I groan out. "You were there when I nearly knocked her ass over tit, remember? That was our meet-cute." I laugh, shaking my head. "Anything else I can do for you?" I roll my eyes as I continue my leisurely stroll toward the gallery.

"Was this your first date? You know, since…" her voice trails off, and my feet stop moving.

In an instant my mood changes. I hang my head and kick at the snow on the sidewalk with my boot. "It wasn't a date, Sophia. I shouted a beautiful woman lunch after humiliating her in a crowded café."

Snow starts to fall harder, and I retreat to the nearest shelter which is the overhang out in front of a woman's clothing store. That's when I see it.

The sign in the window reads, 'Get the Kassidy

Look.' The mannequin wears a beanie with a matching scarf wrapped around its neck. The tag on both shows the Kassidy Lane logo.

Fuck the universe.

"Jarett, you there?" Sophia's voice brings me into the present again.

"Yes, yes, I'm here. You were saying?"

I turn away from the shop window to concentrate on my sister's incessant need for information.

"I *said*, is she coming for drinks with us tonight?"

I already told her we'll be there.

"She is. I'm taking her to dinner first. We'll meet you guys there at the normal time." I pause to weigh the meaning of this, and Sophia laughs.

"So not a date," she chides through the phone.

Again, I roll my eyes.

"Goodbye, Sophia!" I groan once more, a common response to my interfering older sister.

"Wait!" she yells. "I'm taking the mickey, brother. Date or no date, you shared lunch with a woman today. A gorgeous woman. I want to make sure you're okay mentally and emotionally."

I close my eyes and tilt my head upward, allowing the flow of mixed emotions to coarse through me. "It's not like I've never seen a beautiful woman before, Soph."

"I'm aware, but..." Her words haunt me, and neither of us wants to acknowledge it.

My Five Night Fling

"There have been others, so stop overthinking this." My patience with this call is withering away, and my words were growing sharp.

"Don't bullshit a bullshitter, bro."

I give up.

"See you both tonight," she adds and ends the call.

The gallery is my safe place where I can focus on the art, the beauty of the world, and allow all else to fall away. Sometimes I stand in front of my artwork and the pieces of others I commission for hours, alone, while imagining a different life dwelling on the beauty of the art.

Picturing life as it should've been.

Acknowledging the pain, knowing it was never as I believed it to be.

And it never will be.

Lindy, my receptionist of nine years, greets me from the front desk as I breeze past her toward my office—to the place I love, the room where I do my best work—both creatively and in business. "Good afternoon, sir," she sing-songs and hurries over to me with a pile of messages.

"Why are you so damn happy?" I grumble.

"Your morning meeting may not have been as disastrous as you first assumed." Her eyes twinkle as she palms the notes off to me and skips over to her desk.

I flick through the handwritten phone messages on my way upstairs. It appears the buyer I met with this morning has reconsidered and is willing to come to the party with my offer. This is a welcome distraction and puts a bounce in my step after my call with Sophia.

I lock myself inside my sanctuary to return the calls, set another few meetings for next week, and return the call to the dealer from this morning.

I end the conversation feeling pumped. I've been trying to secure this new business relationship for months, and the scales have finally tipped in my favor.

We should expect a brand-new shipment of first-class portraits to fill our walls right in time for next month's gallery showing. These were the events used to pull in the most cash and cement new relationships with dealers and buyers.

I peer at the portrait on my wall and reminisce of a time I spent in the drawing-room with the stunning beauty in front of me. Elegantly displayed and semi-naked, I sketched her magnificence. It was the last time I did a live sketch.

It was the last time I created anything.

For the first time since the accident, my pulse quickens at the idea of standing before a blank canvas and pouring my soul into new work. It's time to move forward and re-engage in my craft. It was once the thing I lived for, but subsequently, it died along with my greatest love.

My artistic ability is the one thing, the one love which will never be taken from me. The desire to create or not is completely in my control.

The chance meeting with Kassidy today ignited a spark that had dimmed so much, it had become non-existent. Sophia is right to call me a bullshitter. I haven't entertained a woman for dinner or sexual gratification since my world fell apart. Nor was it on my agenda to ever do so again.

Until now.

I can't ignore the natural flow of events.

The old Jarett is swooping in, the confidence and charm I once had—it's still there—I had simply buried the fucker beneath the pain of loss and emotional torment.

I run my fingers around the edge of the frame holding the seductive portrait in place opposite my desk. I allow the memories to flow through my mind and try to ignore my pending date tonight, one I unconsciously agreed to with Kassidy.

Prompted by my meddling sister.

Soulful eyes glare at me from the canvas, and I

imagine her lips turning upward into her signature smile.

At this moment, I sense her approval in moving on.

In moving forward.

For I have no other choice but to live the life she and I never could.

Chapter 5

KASSIDY

The small but tidy room overlooks the River Thames with the London Eye, the central attraction. Jarett promises it will be a beautiful sight at night, lit up against the city sky.

I'm thrilled about exploring the beauty and history of London over the next few days. First, I need to unpack and crawl into the tiniest shower I've ever laid eyes on.

As I prep the water, increasing the temperature as much as I dare, I ponder the possibilities of the evening. I'm certain a night with Jarett will be one worth experiencing. A one-night stand to challenge all others and potentially shape my view of men long into the future.

My body shakes with expectation as I step beneath the spray.

Tonight may end up being a life-altering opportunity, at least for me. Normally, I'm the one to fuck random men on a whim to satisfy a need. Always the one to sneak out when sleep takes them, having already forgotten the source of attraction.

I have a feeling the early hours of tomorrow morning might slay the norm.

At least, I hope it will.

Hot water sprays over my hair and flows down my body, soothing the aches and pains. If I were not concerned about falling asleep and drowning, I'd submerge myself in the tub, but that will have to wait until tomorrow.

I allow my head to rest against the shower wall, needing the support to stay upright. Enjoying the intensity of the water pressure falling over my chest, I beam, thinking of Jarett and the effortless way he pulled me to him and kissed me before he left. As if it were the most natural thing in the world.

Me, on the other hand, I almost forgot to breathe. He caught me by surprise, sucked the air from my lungs, and brushed my lips with the most tender of kisses. Anything more, and I'd have fallen to my knees in a puddle.

My body responds to him in ways I had forgotten were possible in the presence of another person.

With the kiss fresh in my mind, my fingers descend over my stomach until I reach the needy spot between my legs. I'm glad I took care of grooming last night because I simply don't have it in me right now.

An ache so old my body fails to register it any longer, was fueled by a stunning stranger today. A man who portrays my desired bad-boy image with a glimpse of a successful entrepreneur.

Family orientated too and will satisfy any parent's prerequisites. Over lunch, Jarett spoke of losing his parents at a young age. Despite this, it's evident his family imparts strong qualities and values that will make any woman proud to be at his side.

But his qualities aren't the part of him I want.

His values, not the part of him I yearn for.

Neither of those causes my clit to throb.

Dangerously, my clit isn't the only part of my anatomy responding to Jarett. I need to keep my wits about me and my walls high. I'm not interested or willing to let my heart out to play. This visit is purely for physical pleasure.

A chance to destress.

Unwind.

Revel in a new city, rich history, and worldly entertainment.

I recall why I'm here. I can't allow my heartstrings to sway in the wind like all my girlfriends back home.

Nope, not me.

Five nights.

My stay is limited.

I have return flights booked.

I remind myself that whatever this turns out to be, one night or five, I'll be saying goodbye at the end of it all.

In my heart, I already know it will be a risk.

The fun part—it will be a risk worth taking.

Surrounded by steam and barely able to keep my eyes open, I try to recall ever feeling this free. For the first time, nothing is out of reach or off-limits.

Breaking free.

Finally letting go.

Fuck yes, I'm doing this.

I'm not sure what I so desperately want to break free from, but I am ready to soar.

Circling my fingertip over my throbbing clit, I tease myself before sliding my finger through the slick heat of my pussy. I imagine Jarett on his knees before me, fucking me with his eyes.

My body tingles from head to toe under his watchful eye. Heat rushes through my core as he leans forward to replace my fingers with his tongue.

My knees buckle slightly beneath me. With increasing speed, my hand works to bring me closer to a release. Sleep will evade me while I'm on fire like this, but I need this.

Rocking backward and forward to my rhythm, I push two fingers deep inside my pussy. Fuck, I'm so wet. My spare hand finds my breast, and my fingers caress my nipples, pulling first at one, then the other. They're hard enough to cut ice.

In my mind's eye, Jarett scrapes his teeth over the hardened points. Sensations flow through my body, one mixing with the next until I'm unsure where one starts and the other ends.

I picture Jarett's hands massaging my inner thighs as he buries his face between them. Oh, how I need to pull at his dark wet hair and ride his face until I come. I'm so close. I can't wait to grope his body and have him grind intimately against me.

Writhing against my hand, Jarett right there with me, I use my thumb to apply the perfect pressure on my clit, tipping me over the edge. A sharp tweak of my nipple pushes me further off the cliff. His name falls from my lips as I ride myself beyond the tormented pleasure.

Nothing will satisfy my need for him.

I'm in so much trouble.

And Jarett, he's in for the ride of his life.

On shaky legs, I step out of the shower, dry off and wrap my hair in my towel. I find a small jug in the kitchenette to make a hot cup of chamomile tea before I fall asleep.

I consider calling my girlfriends in Australia before the time difference pulls me up short. It's the middle of the night for them, and now Chloe and Raven are joined at the hips with their lovers, I don't want to interrupt their sleep.

I'm sure Miah would answer my call immediately, but I'd prefer to speak with them all at once, so I send a text with a quick video of the view from my window and promise to call them tomorrow.

I draw the curtains to bathe the room in darkness.

With no television in the room for noise, I plug my phone into the charger and select a relaxing playlist while I sit in bed with my tea.

After a few sips, my eyelids flutter, struggling to stay open. I pull back the covers and dive between the crisp, clean sheets. Cold against my nakedness, I sink deeply into the mattress and pull the covers to my chin, chasing the warmth.

Absolute bliss.

Reaching over to retrieve the chamomile tea bags from my mug, I take each one and place them gently over each eye. The deep dark circles beneath them screaming out with pleasure.

Five hours later, my alarm sounds, waking me from

a solid slumber. My skin is flushed from being wrapped so tightly in the plush comforter.

I have less than one hour to spare until Jarett arrives. I knew if I didn't set the alarm, I would have slept through the evening.

Once I complete my makeup and I'm happy with the seductive vibe emanating back at me in the mirror, I gawk wistfully at the open closet. What is a girl to wear in London amidst the snow and still ooze sex appeal?

Dressed-to-kill is the look I'm going for.

Not an easy feat with the limited outfits at my disposal. As much as I hate it, a shopping spree was out of the question to avoid excess luggage on my way here. The one item I was unable to resist when in New York, on my way to Prague, is my *only* choice for tonight. It's an easy-on, easy-off satin slip-gathered dress.

Smooth and delicate.

Seductive and adorable.

I shimmy into the dress and shake my bootie in the mirror. The dark silver satin falls freely over the natural curves of my body. It will work perfectly with my sensual moves on the dance floor.

Mind you, I was born with a negative dose of rhythm, but I've never let it stop my natural desire to move to the beat. Where alcohol is involved, I'm never one to stay seated. Dancer or not—seductive or damn awkward—I'll always be found on the dance floor.

Often, up close and personal with at least one irresistible hottie.

Tonight, my preference is one.

Mr. Jarett Evans.

Turning side-on in the mirror, I admire the little New York number landing midway over my sculpted thigh. The hemline accentuates the effort I've put in at the gym lately. In the best shape of my life, I hope I've found the perfect man to worship every part of me.

With the diamante-encrusted neck of the dress, bling is unnecessary. Glancing at my phone, I suspect Jarett will be knocking at the door any minute.

My sky-high heels glide effortlessly over my pantyhose, hugging my legs securely. Fingers crossed, the heel is stable enough for walking on the snow-covered ground. Lord, help me if there are stairs where we're going.

"Just a minute," I yell moments later when a knock at the door demands my attention.

Crap, earrings.

I race into the bathroom in search of my diamond hoops, an expensive and out-of-the-ordinary graduation gift to myself when I finished my degree at the top of my class. I thread the sparkling hoops through my lobes with shaky fingers, taking a second to center myself.

Quickly, I apply another coat of gloss, smack my lips together loudly, and chuckle as I walk toward the door.

"Coming," I announce again.

Nervously, I run my hands across the front of my dress as I approach the door and fling it open.

Holy sweet fuck.

Chapter 6

KASSIDY

Cover model alert. At my door.

How is it possible he looks hotter than he did six hours ago?

I take my time as my eyes caress him from the feet up before locking with his.

"Wow, Kassidy," he gasps, remaining in the hall. "You're absolutely beautiful."

No words justify the relief rolling over me at hearing his words.

"Come here." Jarett clutches my waist and pulls me toward him. "I hope you didn't believe for one second I'd regard you as anything less than beautiful," he whispers. He cups my chin ever so delicately, in complete contrast to the way he pulled me in. And I love it. Then he tilts my head, so my eyes remain invested in his, and he leans over me until his warm breath mingles with mine.

Our lips meet for a prolonged yet too-short moment.

It was a safe kiss.

I need more.

So much more.

My pulse quickens.

"Mesmerizing," he purrs in my ear.

I pull away, grinning at his compliment. "You scrub up pretty decent yourself, Mr. Evans."

Jarett captivates me in ways words can't explain. As much as I want to show Jarett the true me, the one whose confidence never waivers, a giver of no fucks, all things I sense he appreciates in a woman, I stand in his presence like a stale puddle of sticky, gooey mess.

In the face of adversity and the eye candy before me, I hold my head high.

"You can drop *Mr. Evans* unless the occasion calls for it."

My insides do a backflip when he winks at me.

Lord have mercy on my soul.

"It was lovely of your sister to invite me tonight. I hope it's not an overstep on her part or mine for agreeing to go."

Jarett chuckles. "Technically, you didn't agree. I accepted for you and hoped you wouldn't shoot me down in flames."

I fetch my long fake-fur coat and clutch.

"You and Sophia have similar tastes in fashion," he continues as he helps me into my coat.

"I'm sure she'll love an excuse to take you shopping. I'll arrange it for you tonight."

I'm positive Sophia and I will have many things in common, and shopping will only be one way to fill our time.

Approaching the hotel entrance, Jarett pulls me closer to him as if he knows what's coming. Nothing can prepare me for the small group of onlookers with their camera phones out, snapping photos of us as we step into the street.

"Fucking hell," Jarett snaps. "Keep your head down," he warns.

"Umm, what the fuck was that all about?" I question once the craziness is behind us, and we're sure we aren't being followed.

"Plonkers bored with their life," he insists.

The snow has ceased, but the chill factor has increased ten-fold since lunch. With the darkness comes a depth of cold I'm not accustomed to. My body quivers at the intrusion of the frigid air against my face, and I welcome Jarett's arm around my shoulder. I snuggle into his side, where I fit perfectly.

"Why were they taking photos of us?" I stop abruptly and look at him, waiting for an answer.

Jarett sighs and takes my hand, turning toward me.

"The quick version is this. When my parents died, they left a small fortune behind from their investments. As young, orphaned children, we became the youngest billionaires in Europe."

As I register his words, my eyes bug, and my mouth falls open. "Billionaires?"

"That exasperated look is exactly what I was hoping to avoid."

"Sorry, my bad. I'm shocked, is all."

"Because you never would've picked me as a wealthy Brit?"

I shrug, indifferent. "No, never."

"Now you know why I refuse to wear suits, don't have an on-call driver or any other so-called billionaire luxuries. I've no desire to lessen my family name or memory of my parents by exuding a rich and pretentious lifestyle."

"Makes sense. So, commoners take pictures of you to flaunt your personal life? For money or fame, or both?"

"Fortunately, I have no idea, nor do I give a fuck. When it affects other people, that's when it pisses me off."

"Got it. I have no fucks to give, so don't worry about me. I only hope if any photos of me are published, I look fucking hot, and I'm not in any compromising situations."

Satisfied with the conversation, we continue to our destination for dinner.

Jarett laughs. "I can see the headlines now, *Billionaire Evans snags Aussie Bombshell*."

We walk hand in hand along the river and past the London Eye. What a glorious sight it is all lit up. A happy buzz is all around us, people enjoying their evening, spilling out of the restaurants and lining up for the popular central tourist attractions.

When we make it to the subway, Jarett tells me about the quaint little restaurant he found not too long ago in Soho and promises I'll enjoy it.

I haven't laughed this hard in years. Jarett is playful and full of life. At least on the outside. There are fleeting moments I recognize hidden layers of emotional vulnerability. I guess being orphaned at a young age will have that effect.

Even in the twelve hours I've known him, the value he has brought to my life is immeasurable.

Through dinner or tea, as Jarett likes to correct me, he charms me effortlessly, touching me with flirty gestures at every opportunity. When we arrive, Jarett orders a handful of sample plates, promising to give me a solid taste of what, in his words, 'all tourists should try when they visit London.'

Struggling with a mouthful of black pudding, I focus on his devilishly handsome grin as he explains what I'm eating. He laughs hysterically when I curse him around the undesirable texture and force myself to swallow. I taste eel for the first and last time, devour a spoonful of spotted dick, enjoy a small serving of toad in a hole with gravy and mash, a scotch egg, and Haggis. Another dish I could have lived without. I'm stuffed and well-acquainted with British cuisine.

"Where to now?" I ask as we walk through the streets of downtown Soho.

"A ten-minute subway ride across to Shoreditch," Jarett answers, taking my hand in his. "We're going to dance off all the fabulous food and enjoy some of the best cocktails in London." He unleashes his cunning grin. "You down?"

"I should tell you now, this girl..." I emphasize, pointing at my chest, "... she's got no rhythm, but I still plan on dancing circles around you, though." We both laugh and continue to chat until our next stop.

Oops.

Except for one moment where I lose myself in him.

Unashamedly.

It starts with an innocent kiss, the thank-you-for-a-beautiful-dinner kind of kiss. But my body insists on getting closer to Jarett and shows no signs of patience. When he pulls away after the friendly kiss, I capture his face in my hands, the stubble on his cheeks itching my palms. My mind instantly detours to his face between my thighs. I'm sure my cheeks flush at the visual—maybe he worries I'm hesitating, I don't know—but he leans in and devours my lips with his.

His strong arms wrap around me. Our lips hungry for each other's, I hold his face to mine, our tongues exploring, tasting, and pleasuring. He murmurs into my mouth as his hand wanders to the nape of my neck, and fingers glide through my hair. When he fists my hair, pulling tightly at the roots, it's my turn to purr into our kiss.

My hands drop from his face and duck inside his jacket. Our kiss continues, more intense until I'm ready to swing my legs over his thighs and ride him to Shoreditch. Sadly, our ride stops, and I plummet back to earth.

Sheepishly, I retreat from his hold, feeling like a horny teenager on the school bus. I run my fingers through my hair to bring it to order as he pulls his coat closed to cover the bulge in his jeans. He growls at me. "I've been walking around hard all fucking night."

The kicker?

He has no idea how fucking wet I am right now.

And I can't wait to show him.

Is it unfair to hope we can meet up with his sister and friends for a couple of quick drinks, a dance or two, and sneak out the back?

We enter through a heavy wooden door, leave our coats in the closet area, and descend the narrow staircase into the speakeasy.

Damn these heels. I cling to Jarett as we spiral to the bottom. Modern jazz wafts from the room, and the ambiance created by the dull lighting over the lounge area is invigorating. The scene is both romantic and inviting. Couples and groups dine off to the side while others mingle at the low-seated lounges and royal chaises.

It's like stepping back in time. The rich red furnishings and vintage décor are enhanced by the suspended lighting and extravagant chandeliers hanging from the copper ceilings. The place is exquisite.

I spot Sophia seated at the bar talking to a woman mixing drinks and pouring them into large pineapple mugs, garnishing them with large chunks of fruit and sparkling dust to serve. My eyes widen at the idea of drinking something so decadent.

Jarett takes my hand and guides me toward Sophia. "Hey, Max." Jarett waves at the woman behind the bar, and her face lights up when she spots him.

"About time, Jarett." She beams. The pleasant

surprise quickly turns to one of shock as her eyes follow his hand to where it's wrapped softly around mine. Instinctively, I try to pull away, but Jarett doesn't release his hold on me until Sophia jumps off her stool to offer me a hug.

"Kassidy, hi." She kisses both cheeks alternatively and pulls out a stool next to hers, inviting me to sit. Jarett takes a seat on the other side of me as Sophia takes care of the introductions.

"Maxine, this is Kassidy. We met today at Zest," she explains, looking quickly at Jarett before continuing. "Kassidy is visiting from Australia for a few days."

"Nice to meet you, Kassidy. Welcome to my speakeasy," she offers with a grin, extending her hand over the bar. I peruse my surroundings briefly as I reciprocate.

"As in *your* speakeasy?" Sophia did mention a friend owned it, but Maxine looks so young. Badass, but definitely on the younger side.

Her grin grows into a full-blown smile as Sophia and Jarett both nod in agreement.

Jarett pipes in, "Hence, the name *Maximum*. It's *one* of the most popular cocktail bars in the world. Max built this baby from the ground up going on ten years ago. It wins numerous awards every year." He picks up the glass of whiskey Max pushes across the bar to him and raises it to her with a nod.

A proud and supportive friend.

Another green tick in my book.

"World-class cocktails known for their extensive garnishes and a strange mix of flavors, they are weirdly unique and unapologetically delightful," she boasts and slides two pineapple jugs to Sophia and me.

I don't care what's in it, the drink is served fit for an advertising campaign. Not a drink one would order to demolish, especially on a school night. I accept gratefully and relish my first sip. I open my eyes to all three sets peering at me in suspense.

"The best damn cocktail I've ever had the pleasure of tasting," I assure her. "Hands down." All three laugh at my wide-eyed declaration.

"So, you're here through the weekend only, Kassidy?" Maxine asks, cleaning up her workstation. "Unfortunately, yes. On the first flight out Monday morning."

"Great, I expect we'll have a chance to get to know each other if Jarett is willing to share, that is."

I follow her eyes to where his hand rests on my upper thigh. It's so natural being with him I'm not aware of his touch. I start to respond, but Sophia jumps in, beating me to it.

"We'll see you at the end of shift like usual. I'll make sure she doesn't take off in the meantime." She jabs me playfully with her elbow.

"I'll be here."

Although I have no idea what I'm agreeing to.

The music from the live band behind us, mixed with the lush sweet-and-sour concoction of the cocktail before me, makes my body want to move.

It's invading my soul as if I were floating on a cloud.

"The late crowd is starting to flow in now, so I best get a move on. Enjoy yourselves and see you back here in a bit." She points off to the side of the bar, opposite where the diners were steadily finishing up their meals. "Your booth is free and ready to go."

Moments later, the others arrive. Damon, the gobby wingman I met earlier at Café Zest, along with Leon, another friend of theirs who obviously has a thing for Sophia. Lust oozes from his skin with every secret glance in her direction. And, of course, Roman, who is looking dapper in his denim and button-down with an upturned collar.

If Jarett looks anything like Roman in ten years, my God.

My heart.

Once the introductions and greetings cease, the newcomers order their favorite drinks, and we move to the booth. Royal red velvet, high-back bench seats slope around a large curved wooden table with battery-operated candles in the center.

Seated between Jarett and Sophia, I'm comfortably intrigued. I engage in conversation as much as possible, but with their accents together with the music, I admit I am often unsure whether I'm laughing or responding at the right times. Nobody seems to mind, so I continue soaking up the ambiance.

"Are you okay?" Jarett whispers after my eyes have been roaming for a beat too long.

"Yes." I smile as I bring my drink to my lips and sink further into the lounge. "I'm taking everything in. It's quite the place."

"I can't argue with you there, but the view from where I'm sitting is the best." His eyes roam from my face to my thighs and up again. I want so badly to kiss him, hell, rip his clothes off, but instead, we gaze silently at each other until we're interrupted with another round of drinks.

"Now, this is a drink," Sophia oohs and aahs, passing the fishbowl to me. It's more of a fucking meal than a drink. This place is insane. I'm speechless. Probably for the best as I don't fancy offending anyone unintentionally.

Sophia shares the mix with me. Coconut, cacao, Havana Club, beer-roasted feijoas, and wait for it— banana bread, topped with a huge peanut butter ice cube. My mouth plunges in awe.

My reaction is comical to the rest of the table, but I'm beginning to question how one should walk home after all this food and drink.

"Trust me..." Jarett warns, "... you need the bread to soak up the alcohol. Those things are potent.

Sure to get you plastered."

"Oh, I understand what's happening here," I tease, taking another sip. "You're purposely trying to get me drunk and seduce me." I fake horror at the scandal of it all.

He laughs and pulls me in for a kiss. And I let him.

Fuck yes. He owns these lips tonight.

I want him with every fiber of my womanly self.

Chatter around the table lulls as we share the moment, or they simply fade into the background as I bask in the presence of this gorgeous man.

It's an odd feeling to be so comfortable with a man I've barely known for a day. I promise myself not to dwell on this fact. I'm here to enjoy every single moment to the best of my God-given ability.

And I will.

I dared to taste-test the shit out of every single cocktail brought to the table, and each one laid in front of me is taken away empty. I should be full to my toes, but instead, I'm bouncing with energy and slightly intoxicated.

Jarett and I share a dance or two on the makeshift dance floor and immerse ourselves in the band. Not once do I trip, and never does he mention my love-hate relationship with rhythm. We sway in each other's arms and jive to the upbeat songs like teenagers at the prom.

When we return to the group after the set finishes for the night, our last drinks are ready and waiting. When I don't believe these things can get any more decadent, I'm amazed.

Truly. Each one outshines the last.

A cocktail glass with a blue crystal pyramid with smoke billowing from it has my name written all over it. And holy fuck, I need a few glasses of water after this baby if I'm expected to climb those stairs in the next few hours.

The mood settles as Maximum closes for business, and Max joins us with a few sample liqueurs. The complimentary plate of Mexican-style tapas prepared by the chefs help to sober my ass nicely.

When we make it out of here, my focus is seducing Jarett. I'm not about to fail on the libido front.

An hour later, my anticipation heightens as we near the apartment block on foot. Jarett suggests we stay at his home away from home as it was late. I don't want to inconvenience him by escorting me to my room and having to return home to prepare for work a few hours later, so I agree.

Against my better judgment.

If he doesn't live up to my expectations, I may want to pee and flee in the wee hours of the morning.

Chapter 7

KASSIDY

Scanning the apartment, it's similar to any place you'd rent for a night. It's spotless and stylish but severely lacks personality, even for a bachelor pad. The living area is a spacious open plan and two bedrooms and a bathroom are down the hall. There are no photos, trophies, keepsakes, or anything personal at all.

A rug under the coffee table, two cushions, and a throw on the sofa are the only décor items I see as I stand in the center of the room, except for an abstract painting in various shades of purple.
It hints at pain and torture but not the terrifying kind. It weeps heartbreak and suffering. An odd piece to have in a bachelor pad.

Jarett is in the expansive kitchen pouring a glass of wine each.

"You alluded to this being your home away from home. Do you stay here often, or is this your safe place to, you know, bring women?" I probe, smiling at him as he approaches with my wine.

He scoffs.

"Thank you." I take my glass and follow his lead, relaxing on the sofa beside him.

"I've never brought a woman here," Jarett denies, quietly rubbing his chin. I wait for him to elaborate, unsure how to respond.

Suddenly, Jarett's attention dives. He seems to withdraw, and his eyes become distant.

I lift the glass of wine to my lips as he spins to face me and tucks his leg beneath him, creating a barrier of sorts between us. "I purchased this place about six months ago. I guess I was searching for a change of scenery."

He chuckles softly and rubs at the base of his neck. "I'm having a tough time leaving the past behind, so I leave a few changes of clothes in the closet, the basic personal shit, and occasionally stay so it appears lived in."

I nod as if I understand his dilemma, but I have no advice to offer without knowing what he's struggling to leave behind, nor is it my place to advise.

What if he suffered a bad breakup recently, and I'm his rebound? Regardless, who am I to pry?

Something about his discomfort during the

conversation makes my heart hurt for him.

I scan the room for the television, thinking some background noise might help alleviate the awkward silence. The problem is, this is a television-free zone.

Maybe he has one in the bedroom.

Jarett catches me searching the room. "Yeah, I need to make the place more homely, huh?"

"It will happen in time. When you're ready to make it yours," I offer sincerely.

"Music." He grabs his phone and scrolls through Spotify to find a playlist.

Thank fuck.

"Sorry, I guess I kinda brought the vibe down a tad."

I feign indifference with a shrug. "It's been a long day, don't worry about it." I place my hand on his knee. "It's been a hell of a good day, though, and an even better night. I honestly can't thank you enough, Jarett."

He covers my hand with his own, giving it a firm squeeze. "It's been the best day I've had in the longest time."

Reaching over to take my glass, he sets both on the side table at his end of the sofa. When he turns to me, the sorrow in his eyes has turned to stone-cold lust.

His stare penetrates my fuzzy interior and ignites a fire in the pit of my stomach. His hand brushes my hair over my shoulder, away from my face, and cups my neck. I melt into his touch and allow him to pull me closer, our lips meeting in a lust-fueled kiss.

Our tongues duel slowly in the beginning until our moans grow deeper. Jarett threads his hands through my hair, gripping the roots in his palms.

I move to a kneeling position, my hands running along the length of Jarett's arms, massaging his shoulders as my body is drawn to his like a magnet. My fingers trace the neckline of his shirt all the way down his torso.

I grapple with the hemline of his shirt and peel it up his body and over his head as I climb over him, positioning myself in his lap. I take his mouth, and his hungry kiss consumes me. His strong hands snake their way beneath my dress, and he unclips my bra. Strapless, it falls between us, and he groans, breaking the kiss.

Pulling it free, he flicks it across the room. With his eyes focused on mine, he lifts my dress over my head and drops the flimsy material beside us.

Jarett gushes at the sight of my breasts hanging freely. His hands gently massage each of them simultaneously before he takes a nipple into his mouth. The heat of his lips, mixed with the coolness of being suddenly naked, fuels my libido. My head falls backward as he licks and sucks, alternating between both breasts.

I grip his head and hold him in place, not wanting this tease to end.

But wanting it to end all the same.

I want him all over me.

I need him to explore my body, to worship me.

My desire to also pleasure him is also high on my to-do list.

First night in London, I need to get him out of my system, so I'm free to explore more moments like this over the coming days.

Before I return home to Australia.

Without warning, Jarett grips my ass and holds me to him, standing tall in one swift movement. Two seconds pass between us.

Is he having second thoughts?

As fleeting as the moment is, so is the walk to the opposite end of his apartment. He strides down the hall, kissing my neck, my feet wrapped around his buttocks, both naked from the waist up.

Jarett places me on the bed, stands in front of me, and removes his pants. The room is dark, but with the light filtering in from the hall, the definition of his torso is evident, the muscles in his shoulders rippling as he works my legs free of my boots and pantyhose.

I lay in wait, desperate for his attention and vulnerable beneath his gaze.

His eyes travel upward from my toes, lingering on my panties. I send up a silent thank you to the lingerie gods of this world. I observe him as he swallows, the heat in his eyes liquefying my body. His nostrils flare, his chiseled jaw takes on a hardness I haven't seen before. Slowly, he reaches for my thong, loops his fingers in the sides, and tears it from my body.

Unexpectedly, I shriek. Jarett brings the torn remnants of lace to his nose and inhales deeply. My pulse quickens as I lay here, taking in the sight of this man I need more than I've wanted any other human in my life.

Quickly, he releases the button on his jeans and shoves the denim past his thighs, leaving him completely exposed to me.

Mmm, commando is definitely my type.

I gulp at the sight of him as he steps out of his pants and tosses my panties on the floor. His eyes roam my body before they land on my treasure chest of glistening jewels. I enjoy the show of him stroking his cock slowly.

My thighs clench, anticipating his size and the pleasure I'm undoubtedly about to endure.

I wasn't counting on not being able to walk tomorrow, but fuck, I'm not complaining.

Finally, Jarett approaches the bed, his knees supported at the edge, and grabs both of my feet, positioning them further apart until I'm completely open and exposed to him. Hunger radiates from him, his eyes dark and hooded with lust.

My breath hitches as he lowers his face between my thighs and... fuck.

This guy.

Sliding his hands beneath my ass, he palms both cheeks and gives them a hard squeeze. My hips writhe and lift from the mattress to meet his tongue as it runs through my folds from the bottom to the top. His tongue flicks rapidly over my clit, and he lavishes my nerve endings with the warmth and wetness of his mouth. Lips encompass my swollen lady boner, and he sucks. Hard.

I let out a heavenly sigh and clench the life out of the comforter with my hands. I force my body to stay still, not to give in to my desire.

It's a hopeless effort—this man's mouth is made to be ridden.

I chase my orgasm as if it's the last chance I'll ever have to satisfy my need. I follow it to the ends of the earth until my whole world shudders and quakes beneath me before toppling over the edge into a satiating abyss.

"Fucking hell, you taste heavenly, Kassidy."

It doesn't end. Satisfaction encases me, and I'm falling deeper into the bed as the moments pass, yet those words dripping from his lips ignite a deeper passion in my soul.

After rolling a condom over his length, Jarett crawls over my body until the head of his cock is tapping my entrance. I'm so fucking wet, my orgasm mixed with his saliva, I can't resist raising my pelvis slightly until I feel him beginning to enter me.

Stretching me.

The most incredible, lip-smacking intrusion of my thirty years.

On my first night in the Big Smoke, I'm reduced to red-hot ambers of lust.

"Christ, Kassidy." Jarett's body is shaking above me. His need is as uncontrollable as my own.

He continues to fill me slowly. I clutch his ass and drive his hips forward.

"Fuuuck," he whispers raggedly, holding still above me. "Careful, sweetheart, you might get more than you bargain for." His eyes penetrate mine as he finally moves.

The air between us swirls together, our breathing harsher with each stroke of his cock hitting me deeper inside. I allow my eyes to drift close, and my head falls further into the bed, my chest rising. His tantalizing mouth is on me again, caressing my hardened nipples.

Finding our rhythm, he palms my breasts as he kisses his way across my exposed neck, leaving a heated trail of desire to my mouth. My eyes spring open as he pulls my chin forward and devours my lips.

The bed bounces beneath us, and the world closes in around us until there's only him. And me.

Together.

As one.

On the edge of my second orgasm, he pulls out and flips me to my stomach. Positioning my knees closer to my waist and at a wider angle apart, he props me perfectly in line with his cock. I cry out as he enters me again.

Deeper than before.

His hands find my breasts bouncing beneath me and uses them to secure his body to mine as he continues to pound into me. Each movement is driving me further into the headboard until I have no choice but to extend my head backward.

Thank fuck for yoga and the inverted cat poses.

Jarett rises with me, his hand bracing the front of my throat. I push myself deeper into his palm, willing him to tighten his grip. Our bodies mash together, sweat pools between us, my ass cheeks slapping his thighs an echo in the stillness of the night.

I'm completely aware of every muscle in his body, the cologne he wears infiltrating my sensory system, the droplets of exhaustion landing on my shoulders as sweat drips from his hairline.

"You want me to choke you, sweetheart? Is that what you want?"

I nod.

Words evade me.

"Tell me, Kassidy." His hands squeeze me harder

for a millisecond, and he releases me.

Teasing me.

Riling me up.

"Harder." It's all I manage to say.

Both his hands grip my throat, and his palms pull tighter across the front of my throat until my airway constricts slightly.

Exactly what I need.

Everything I want.

My need fuels him.

He pumps into me from behind, pulling me by the neck harder over his cock, threatening to break me wide open.

Like he has done with my desire.

Opening a can of what-the-fuck, I'm going to need more than tonight.

I want it.

More.

Of him.

"Come for me, baby," he growls in my ear, and it's all the encouragement I need. I let go, screaming out with the overwhelming pleasure this man provides. He gives in to his release seconds after me, and together we collapse on the bed.

In the silence of the night, I lay awake listening to Jarett's breathing become steadier until it evens out, and it's evident he's fallen asleep.

Chapter 8

KASSIDY

I wake up on the sofa in Jarett's shirt, the sunlight shining through the window. Man, traveling fucks with my sleep pattern. I have no idea what time it was when I finally fell asleep, but I crawled out of Jarett's arms at least an hour after he passed out. I was tossing and turning and didn't want to wake him.

Plus, I've never stayed the night with a man before.

Thankfully, I'm on holiday with the freedom of time. I have no idea about his work schedule and timeline, but he does have a gallery to run.

Speaking of which, is he still here?

Surely, he didn't abandon me in his apartment. I search on the floor for my phone until I vaguely remember stumbling around in the dark trying to find the charger in the kitchen. I groan as I push myself up to a sitting position.

My eyes are heavy, and even without a mirror, I can tell my hair is a solid mess. I cringe, knowing I have to make it back to my room in this state. It's a damn good thing I have no chance of running into someone I know.

"Morning, you." I run my fingers under my eyes before turning in the direction of his voice to find Jarett in the kitchen.

"Morning," I manage around a yawn. He chuckles at my morning face. "Is that coffee I smell?"

"Figured you might need some," he offers as I pull up a stool at the breakfast bar.

I take the mug he offers and inhale the scent of strong morning coffee—my lifeblood. No day should ever begin before a coffee or three.

"I guessed it! You're a coffee addict."

I raise my eyebrows at his observation, taking a hearty sip of the frothy warmness. "You inhaled it as if it were your drug of choice. Only an addict smells their product before trying it." I can't help but chuckle at his logic.

He observes me while I sit silently enjoying my caffeine hit.

"Was it the bed or me you were escaping from early this morning?" he asks openly. It takes a moment to respond, so he continues, "I was worried when I woke up that you might have been gone."

I shake my head, my bed hair bobbing around heavily at the movement. "Nope, wasn't leaving. I couldn't sleep and didn't want to disturb you."

He nods at my response but offers nothing further, and an awkwardness spikes between us. Looking at my phone, it's a little after eight, and I have messages from Chloe, Raven, and Miah.

"I should head off, change, and take in some of this beautiful city."

I don't wait for a response, so I excuse myself to the bathroom to change and tie my hair in a messy bun. Thankfully, my long coat will hide the fact I'm still in last night's clothes.

Jarett is ready to go when I walk out.

"We may as well travel together. I need to go to the gallery to take care of some business. Did you want to meet there when you're ready? I'll give you a tour. And we should have a gander at some tourist attractions. I'm up-to-date on all the best places and may be able to get you cheaper rates." He smirks, his eyebrows raised in question.

Or hope.

The only answer is yes.

I can't deny spending more time with Jarett. He's high on my list of wants. "Sounds perfect." I grin, glad the growing silence from earlier has now dissipated.

Chapter 9

KASSIDY

"I met a guy. He's sexy as fuck, successful, and set on showing me around the city." I walk around the room getting ready for the day while speaking with Miah on FaceTime. "Oh, and he's a billionaire, but who cares, he is adorably sweet and swoon-worthy as hell."

"Meaning you fucked a stranger last night, he was so fucking hot in bed, and you want a round two." She laughs at her cleverness in assessing the situation.

"Yes and no. The sex was off the charts, but…" I scramble into my skinny jeans and layer the top with a thick woolen sweater and scarf.

"Wait, he's a billionaire? What's his name, I'll Google him?"

"Don't you dare," I practically scream at her.

"Killjoy." She huffs. "What's with the but?"

"He's a great guy, the kind of guy you'd take-home-to-your-parents great. The I-feel-like-I've-known-you-forever type."

Miah continues to nod at me with no regard for my dire situation.

"Help a girl out, would ya? You know me, I prefer cock over chatter and his name? Who the fuck cares?"

Miah roars with laughter. "Yes, girl. So, you."

"Well, this is *not* that."

"Oh? But you're leaving in a few days." She sighs sadly.

"Exactly. I'm open to the company and hot sex for the next few days, and I'll fly home, no regrets." The words flow from my mouth but fail to connect where they should.

"Oookay. You keep telling yourself that." The bitch rolls her eyes at me.

Who am I kidding? Not myself and not her, either.

Ending the call, I send a quick text to my mother.

Me: *London is great. Love you.*

On my way to the gallery, I stop to enjoy a big breakfast of bacon with a pancake stack for one and the best beet juice I've ever tasted. For the remainder of the short walk, I order the largest coffee available with a few extra shots.

Now I stand outside the gallery thinking of the day to come until the door opens, and Jarett ushers me inside. "I wasn't sure how long you were going to stand there, but I was beginning to feel uncomfortable watching you," he jokes.

At the reception desk, he introduces me to Lindy and takes my coat. "Thank you."

I scan the area. "You have a coffee shop in here?" I observe, raising my cup.

Once we tour the upper exhibition level and return to the smaller public galleries near the entrance, I stop in front of a sculpture of a Greek god. Beyond the statue are two intimate gallery rooms, much smaller than the others. I start to veer toward them when Jarett subtly urges me in the opposite direction.

He shares the history of the prints lining the walls, and the expanse of artwork is exceptional. Being a modern gallery, it's less about history and culture than aesthetically appealing artistic greatness.

Making no attempt to take me into the room on the left of the Greek god, curiosity gets the better of me. "Is there a reason we're skipping this exhibit?" I ask, pointing to the one area we have not yet toured.

His gaze bounces between me and the entry before giving in. "Sure, why not?" I follow behind him this time as he moves through the gallery at a faster pace. That's when I see the sign at the end of the viewing room. "Jarett Evans' Personal Collection."

"Wait, what?" My legs abruptly stop moving. I eyeball Jarett, "How did I not... artist and billionaire... you're a man full of secrets, aren't you? "Jarett slides his hands inside his pockets and lowers his head.

"Creating art isn't a huge part of my life anymore."

Only twelve pieces line the walls, but they vary from street art, boudoir portraits, and abstract prints. "Wow, this woman is phenomenal. Her beauty is outstanding, and you capture it perfectly. You have a few sketches of her. Is she a model you work with regularly?"

Jarett pauses, avoiding eye contact with me or the portrait I'm referring to. Instead, he turns to the opposite wall filled with large abstract paintings.

"As a digital designer, I'm sure you can appreciate abstract art for the color sequence, depth, and tones. Color speaks a lot to the personality and feelings, like a calling card, I guess. You'd be familiar with this from your marketing experience, yeah?"

We continue to talk about the abstract pieces, but it bugs me he avoided the question about the model. If she is more than a model to him, what will it matter?

I remind myself it's five nights. Lack of personal information isn't a deal-breaker.

Besides, the less personal we are, the better.

The remainder of the day is action-packed. We explore all the main attractions Central London has to offer. We laugh, roam the streets hand in hand, and take ridiculous selfies like a couple in love. I learn so much about the English culture and the history of this beautiful city.

Jarett is the best tour guide.

And true to his word, I saved money on all the entry fees. I guess it pays to be a *someone,* even if you don't want to be. We visit Westminster Abbey, photograph the River Thames and surrounding historical sites from a bird's-eye view on the London Eye, walk the London Tower, and inspect the castles.

We picnic in the park, feed the squirrels, marvel at the swans on the lake, and attend the Changing of the Guards at Buckingham Palace after a group tour inside.

"You look knackered, sweetheart."

"Aren't you? I'm royally fucked."

We both crack up as a woman from a tourist booth approaches us with tickets for a three-course dinner and burlesque show package deal.

My feet ache, my stomach grumbles, and light rain in the past five minutes has made me cold and irritated. But I love burlesque and where better to enjoy it than right here in London.

Jarett produces his wallet without question. "No, please. Let me," I argue, digging into my purse for the paper bills I still can't quite decipher.

"Call me old-school, sweetheart, but if I'm taking you on a date, I'll be making the booking and getting the bill."

Of course, he will.

I'll be sure to thank him later.

We have ninety minutes until seating commences.

"How far from here to my room on foot?"

"Under ten minutes."

"Great, walk with me and wait while I change?"

"My pleasure, sweetheart."

My phone needs charging from all the photos and videos I've taken of our adventures, and there's still so much more to post on Instagram. I have been hash-tagging everything, and my followers have grown over two thousand in less than twenty-four hours.

I was feeling a little *Emily in Paris,* but hey, it's a tourist's prerogative. Priorities first, I charge my phone and sneak in a quick shower.

Pouring my aching legs into my skinny black leather pants and favorite pair of stilettos, I make my outfit pop with a shimmering gold swing top. A touch of product enhances my curls, a fresh coat of makeup, and I'm good to go.

"Wow." Jarett is waiting on the two-seater couch for me when I step out of the bathroom. "Beautiful. And I've never known a woman to get ready in…" he eyes his wrist, "… less than fifteen minutes." He kisses my cheek affectionately. "I'm impressed. In more ways than one."

"You ought to be," I play with him. "Not all women can be this eager to be on your arms."

Jarett's grin widens. He helps me into my coat and offers me his arm.

"I feel I've taken over your life since the moment I stepped off the subway yesterday."

Jarett takes my hand and turns my chin toward him with the other. "Believe me, I don't want to be doing anything else." He leans in slowly, and our lips meet in a soft, sweet exchange. The flavor of our wine and cheese from earlier mixes with sizzling lust. When we pull back, Jarett's eyes are dark and filled with emotion.

"Oh, one sec." I swap my plain Jane earrings to a set of large diamond hoops and add a spray of Black Opium.

"Mmm, what's this?" Jarett swipes the bottle of Opium from my hands and inhales deeply. "I must buy some of this to keep around after you leave."

I roll my eyes at him. "Yes, you must." We both laugh and head out to catch our show and enjoy a meal.

Chapter 10

KASSIDY

The burlesque show is opulent and eccentric. What more can I say?

We enjoyed Mediterranean cuisine and the perfect portions to digest with a bottle of Italian wine.

The show is coming to an end, and the area will soon convert into a nightclub. The more we drink, the more I want to stay and dance. I'm torn between dancing the night away and fucking Jarett's brains out. The show is saucy, and my juices are flowing.

Who am I kidding? I want him more now than I did last night.

We haven't talked about last night or what to expect from the rest of this evening, though.

I search beneath the table in the middle of the dining area facing the stage and cup Jarett's crotch.

His legs immediately relax, widening a little to allow me to caress his package. Through his jeans, his growth is evident. I clench my cheeks tight on the chair to ward off the dancing in my panties.

Damn these pants. I should've worn a dress. I want him to rub my clit under the table with no barriers and get me off while we watch the finale. My senses are heightened as I imagine other diners catching us in the act.

The nightclub is now pumping with people, and new crowds of partygoers continue to flow in. Our bodies grind against each other on the dance floor, and our hands explore each other's bodies as we move to the beat of the music. The lighting is dull with interchanging colors of flashing lights which accentuate the movement and mood of the dancers.

"Cocktail for the lady, please, and a house beer for me." The bartender nods, perusing me head to toe as Jarett orders for us.

"Classic marg, darlin'?" he asks with a thick American accent.

Jarett pulls me closer to him, placing his hand territorially on my shoulder.

"Please," I confirm.

"There's nothing classic about you, darlin'," Jarett rasps in my ear, putting on a southern twang accent. I shake my head at his stupidity.

Our drinks arrive. "Classic with a twist," the young American winks, taking Jarett's cash.

Jarett leads us to a table for two at the side of the dance floor.

"So, what's the twist?" he asks when we take a seat.

Taking a large sip of my drink, I cough and release the straw from between my lips. Jarett coughs into his fist, trying not to laugh.

"Extra lime, double tequila, and a tinge of something spicy?" I lick my lips. Jarett requests a taste, and I happily hand him the glass.

The tang must have hit his throat in the same way, his face contorting as though he's bitten into a fresh lemon.

"You're not wrong. But Mr. America is all kinds of fucked up if he thinks getting you plastered with this spicy concoction will work. There's no way in hell I'm leaving here without you."

I throw my head to the side in exaggeration. "As if I'd let you."

"Get tanked on one drink or…" he teases.

"Stay without you."

My words please him. I love being the cause of his infectious grin spreading across his lips.

Yeah, so my *one-night* plan with Jarett isn't working out so well. I mean, it's amazing, but it doesn't gel with my plan.

My plan for now. This plan called life.

I'm dangerously close to enjoying my time with him *too much*. There's no room for dating and shit in my life. Plus, I leave in a few days.

We dance, we drink—margaritas mostly—which we order from the other bar to avoid more promiscuous drinks and empty flirting.

In the early hours of the morning, exhaustion takes its toll, and thankfully, Jarett is eager to get me out of here.

Hopefully, he wants to get me into bed again.

Either way, I'm ready for us to head back to the hotel.

"Fuck." I jiggle the card into the slot on my door, praying for it to open. Jarett is grinding against my ass while I drunkenly try to get us inside my room.

"Stop it." I giggle, batting his hand away from undoing my pants. "I'm struggling to get us in the fucking door," I slur.

"May I?" he begs, taking the swipe card from me and slipping it in the latch, popping open immediately.

Typical.

The smartass pumps his fist. "Winner!" I groan out loud as I trudge through the door.

Peeling off my coat, I throw my bag and scarf on the sofa and make quick work of removing my boots. Jarett turns down the bed covers and strips naked, his cock already hard and standing at attention.

He stalks toward me and leans past me to collect my scarf.

Stripping out of my clothes with only my bra and panties in place, I turn to see him with my scarf wrapped around his erection. *My scarf will never be the same again.*

"Gonna restrain me with this thing?" I smirk, grabbing him, searching the room for something he can tie me to.

Jarett stares at me, releases his cock from the material, and spins me around. Taking both my wrists, he ties them together, the fabric dancing over my buttocks and the tops of my thighs, causing goosebumps to break out over my body.

"Is this okay?" he whispers, sucking on my earlobe.

"Yes," I pant, desperate to have his hands on me.

Jarett guides me to the small table in the center of the kitchenette and pushes me forward until my top half is splayed over the cold glass top. The chair screeches across the floor, and he brushes against me, his finger lightly tracing over my ass.

When his palm slaps my right cheek, I yelp. The sting ignites a new level of need. I moan into the table, my heated breath fogging the glass. When his hand comes down over my left cheek, I writhe in place, desperate for more.

"You like that, baby?" he whispers as he runs his finger beneath my panties and between my thighs.

"Fucking hell, Kassidy. You're so wet for me already."

Does this guy have no idea how fucking hot he is? A blind woman would be salivating at the mere closeness of him. His entire aura oozes sex, and his voice dripping from his lips promises pleasure.

I moan as he kisses my shoulders and teasingly removes my panties. Pulling them slowly over my thighs, his kisses follow his movements until the lace falls to my ankles, and he's kneeling below me on the floor.

Beginning at my feet, his hands caress the lengths of my legs until again, he's teasing my pussy with his fingers, his mouth trailing wet kisses from my thighs to meet the moisture pooling in my center.

"Taste so fucking sweet. Never get enough of you," he growls beneath me. My thighs tremble in anticipation as he uses his fingers to fill me with pleasure.

I love a man who can navigate a woman's body without direction.

The way he fondles me, he's made to order. Just for me.

Intimate.

Tantalizing.

A mix of slow movements and rapid strokes has me grinding against him in no time.

"Jarett," I gasp.

"What do you want, Kassidy?" he growls quietly.

I rotate my hips, his fingers deep inside me now.

"You. I want you, Jarett."

He withdraws his fingers and kisses my sensitive clit before standing and forcing me to face him. Heat floods my cheeks as he raises my face until our eyes meet. There are so many ways to interpret the way he looks at me.

I'm giddy with lust.

He releases my bra and lets my breasts fall freely. My arms pull at the restraints. My fingers itch to trace the ridges of his muscular physique, but it only makes the scarf wind tighter around my wrists.

Jarett lifts me onto the table in a swift one-arm movement. My hands fastened behind me, I'm unable to steady myself as he pulses the head of his cock along my pussy. He rubs himself through the wetness, coating his cock with my juices.

"Fuck," he grumbles, leaving me to dig through his jeans for a condom from his wallet. Patience or lack thereof threatens to derail my cool decorum as my eyes fasten on him, watching as he slides the silicone over his length.

Two long strides and he's between my legs again. "Ahh, damn," I gasp as he drives into me in one swift movement. He fills me. So deep. He grips my waist to stop me from falling backward and moves me to meet each of his thrusts until we're both panting. Our moans grow louder.

Not missing a beat, he releases my hands. "Grab

my neck."

He lifts me from the hips and steps away from the table. My inner muscles clench around him as he moves a few feet and spins me around, slamming me into the wall.

He thrusts his hips, pumping into me, driving me up the wall.

Literally. Further with each stroke.

"Kiss me, Kassidy. I need you everywhere."

He moans as I explore his mouth with my tongue. His kisses have a way of reaching depths of me I never assumed possible. I'm so close, but I try to hold off.

"Don't keep it from me, sweetheart. Let me have it," he coaxes me. It tips me over the O-cliff, my fingernails digging into his shoulders as I ride it out.

"Fucking beautiful."

Taking me to the bed, he lays me flat, hooks my thighs over his shoulders, and chases his own release. Like the gentleman he is, he takes me right along with him for the third time.

I barely register moving.

I'm so exhausted, I fall asleep with a man in my bed.

First time for everything.

Chapter 11

KASSIDY

Time passes quickly when you're having fun.

As we clock some decent mileage on foot, my butt muscles scream at me, and the arches of my feet strain to break free from my heeled boots.

After hours of wandering around the markets buying keepsakes and small gifts for Mom, Chloe, Raven, and Miah, we visit a quaint vintage store in Piccadilly Sophia raves about.

Shopping with Sophia is a blast. We both gravitate toward the same things—fashion, jewelry, and décor. I'd given myself this day to lash out on some British fashion to take home.

"Are you limping?" Sophia questions on our way to our next stop, her preferred designer boutique for affordable and chic indie fashion pieces.

"Not intentionally. Apparently, I have muscles in

places I'm not aware of. Your brother and I danced up a storm last night."

I fight to hold off a smile at the memories of the night before. I'm certain not all the muscle aches are from the dance floor.

She eyes me suspiciously as if reading my dirty mind. I ignore the question in her eyes and focus on rectifying my stride. So far, the morning has been a no-Jarett zone, which I appreciate. I sense she wants to ask for details but for whatever reason, hasn't mentioned him.

The past few days and nights have been one hundred percent Jarett-focused, and as fun as it has been, a day without him is good for the soul.

"Let's stop in here for a late lunch." Sophia pauses out front of a hip café with a few spare tables on the sidewalk. The weather is wonderful today—a chill in the air subdued by the sun's warmth sneaking through the soft cloud coverage.

"No need to twist my arm." My feet are begging me to stop.

Once seated, we order our meals, and Sophia finally gives in to resisting the no-Jarett zone.

"So, tell me more about this dancing you and my brother were doing last night," she probes. Her smile is contagious, and I chuckle when she wiggles her eyebrows over her sunglasses.

"Sophia..." I fake gasp and glance around as if I have something to hide. I lean across the table toward her, requesting her full attention. She mirrors my body language and waits on bated breath. "I'm a lady. I never kiss and tell." I push away from the table laughing quietly as her face falls in disappointment.

Cocktails at any time of day, the best thing about vacationing in different cities. The waiter, a hottie if you like the young babyface type, all but drools over Sophia. She shows no interest or even acknowledges his advances in any way.

"Why are you still single?" I ask her directly.

Catching her off guard, she partially chokes on the first sip of her Bloody Mary. "I'm content being single. I am more focused on my career right now, but don't you worry about me, I get all the action between the sheets a good girl like me can want." She winks.

"Do you ever hook up with your clients?"

It's a fair question. At least I thought it was until she squeals, "Kassidy! I would never."

Sophia is an entrepreneur running Europe's largest dating agency. The potential hookups must be endless. Why would she not?

"Really? Never?"

Sophia sighs. "Not never, per se. Occasionally, perhaps. When I have an itch, you know how it is."

I laugh loudly. She cracks me up. "Yeah, I know the itch all too well."

"So seriously, then..." she continues, "... what

have you done to my brother?" Her tone turns serious, and I gulp loudly as I swallow.

"You mean your grown-ass brother who has taken it upon himself to show me around London and turn my few days of rest and relaxation into a fun-filled adventure holiday in one of the greatest cities I've ever visited?"

She shrugs. "Whichever way you look at it... he's completely besotted with you."

I deflect her comment with valor, waving my hand dismissively. "A chance meeting in a café and an opportunity to entertain an Aussie chick for a few days, no strings attached?" I take another mouthful of my spritzer and secretly hope the waiter will be out with our food in record time.

Now she's shaking her head at me, silently laughing. Her chest and shoulders bounce as if she's chuckling, but not a single murmur escapes her.

So, I continue, "Not besotted. A man who oozes charm, a typical ladies' man open to a quick fling." Sophia is quick to jump on me for my observation.

Removing her sunglasses and tucking them into her bag, she reclines into her chair. Crossing her legs and placing both hands, linked together, over her knee, her head drops to the side as she inspects me.

Her stare invades me at a soul level. No exaggeration. The way she glares at me makes my skin prickle and my insides ice over.

Oops!

I've offended her.

Not my intention at all.

I raise my palm to silence her before she lets it rip. "No disrespect, Sophia. Jarett is a wonderful guy, and I've loved every minute of our time together. *Immensely.* But it's all about the fun for both of us. No strings."

Our plates of food are served, and we both remain in a Mexican stand-off.

Her foot begins to bob. a nervous trait or one of annoyance, I'm unsure, but I'd bet my return ticket on the latter. "Here's the thing, Kassidy. I like you. And I love my brother more than anyone or *anything*. But this…" she waves her hand at me, "… whatever it is between you two, is nothing like the Jarett I know."

Officially confused, I frown and lean on the edge of the table, my chin resting on my fists. "I'm sorry, Sophia, I'm not sure—"

Interrupting me, Sophia goes for it. "Jarett has never been a *ladies' man*, as you put it. Charming as hell, *yes*. But he doesn't *play the field* or welcome opportunities to entertain strangers in the bedroom or otherwise."

"Sophia, I've hit a nerve I never intended to." I push my plate to the side and collect my bags, ready to call it a day. My head is spinning. I'm hurt and deflated that this discussion has turned sour.

She lunges forward and places a hand on mine. "Please, don't leave." Her head falls forward, and her eyes slip shut for a few seconds as she inhales deeply. When her eyes meet mine again, they're filled with sadness.

My stomach drops.

I've upset her.

"I'm sorry, Kassidy. My protectiveness of Jarett is often all-consuming and completely displaced. I get it." She lets go of me, and I return my bags to the bench beside me. "I apologize for making you uncomfortable. You're brilliant. Honestly." She shakes her index finger between us. "In the short amount of time I have spent with you, it's like we're sisters from another mother. We have so much in common. I'm the British version of your Aussie one. You get me." She laughs, and I can't resist the genuine grin which spreads across my face because I feel the same way.

"I'm not taking advantage of your brother, I promise... in or outside of the bedroom. It's casual, yes, but I leave in a few days. He's aware of this. And..." I take pause, "... it was you who invited me out my first night here."

Sophia relents. Her shoulders relax, and she exhales dramatically. "You're right, of course. I was so happy to witness Jarett interacting with a woman finally and, well... I figured it would be good for him. You know, after—"

"After?" I ask, following her lead and digging into my crispy fried chicken salad.

Curiosity grips me. *Why is Jarett interacting with a woman so out of the ordinary?*

Sophia analyzes me closely as I enjoy my food, not willing to continue the conversation at this point.

Finishing our food and moving onto our second cocktail each, I press Sophia for more information. The unsettled pocket in the pit of my stomach is causing discomfort. "While we're being open and honest, please, tell me what's on your mind."

Sophia sighs heavily. "After Helena..." *Helena?* "...Jarett completely withdrew, and I worried for a while that he'd never move on. Watching him with you at Café Zest the other day, it's the first time in a year I've truly recognized him. You—" Sophia halts mid-sentence. "Shit, he hasn't talked to you about Helena, has he?"

Nervously, I chew on the inside of my cheek, unsure I should hear this from anyone other than Jarett. If he'd wanted me to know, we'd have talked about it during our time together.

I shake my head, "No, he hasn't."

"Fuck. Me and my big mouth."

"It's fine. We aren't exactly divulging personal information, being a fling and all."

"Kassidy, you've brought him a sense of freedom to live, a desire to let go. And you two are so fucking natural together it's as if fate brought you here, especially for him. And believe me, I don't believe in soppy romance bullshit despite my career choice."

I force out a dry chuckle, "Good, neither do I."

Sophia checks the time on her phone. "We should get moving, but listen, I worry when your time ends here, saying goodbye to you is going to reopen wounds for Jarett. The last time he waved goodbye to someone, it was his wife."

Wife.

Slowly the words sink in.

Jarett is married.

"Jarett is, umm... he's married?" I blurt out.

Sorrow-filled eyes meet mine.

"She never made it home, Kassidy."

I swallow hard, trying to keep my lunch from resurfacing.

"Jarett waved goodbye to her as she boarded a plane to New York for a modeling gig. On her way to the job, she was involved in a major traffic incident." As she speaks, her voice waivers.

My heart breaks for Jarett and all he has been through. Suddenly, the next few days take on a different shape in my mind.

"How tragic, I'm so sorry. I don't know what to say."

As we make our way from the café, Sophia puts her arm around my waist as we walk. "Nothing, sweety, there's nothing to say. I shouldn't have mentioned anything about Helena. I wasn't thinking. I assumed it would've come up between you two at some point. Please do me a favor and don't mention I said anything."

My mood deteriorates rapidly. "Of course."

As the day wears on, we put our earlier discussions behind us, but I can't shake the feeling. Will I be able to look at him the same way and not convey the sadness I feel for him? Ignore knowing his deepest, darkest pain.

As we say goodbye at the subway, each to go our separate ways after a great day out, my phone rings.

The screen lights up.

Jarett.

I silence the call as Sophia hugs me tight. "Please don't brush him off. Despite what you feel or say you do, Jarett would never have bought you lunch if he didn't sense some form of connection with you. Most people live a lifetime without experiencing that."

She lets me go with a solemn smile and walks away.

My heart squeezes, wondering if I'll ever meet with my British twin again. Part of me will miss her as much as Jarett when I leave.

Again, my phone buzzes, but I let it go to voicemail.

Chapter 12

JARETT

"Sophia!" I shout into the phone. Finally, somebody fucking answers me. "I've been calling for ten minutes."

"Chill, baby bro," she huffs. "I was busy unpacking all my new finds from the shops today."

"What have you done to Kassidy?"

"Done to her? What do you mean?" Whatever she was doing in the background fades out, and I have her full attention.

"She's not answering my calls."

"Relax, I not long walked in, so she's likely still en-route to her room."

Right.

I keep telling myself all the things she *might* be doing instead of ignoring my calls on purpose. Like lying dead in the street somewhere, kidnapped by a random subway troll, bludgeoned to death by a modern-day London serial killer. Yeah, none of that's helping.

"Then why isn't she answering her phone?"

"Jarett, stop!" Her abrupt words fall over me in a motherly tone. I know I'm overreacting, but the last time my calls went unanswered…

… I can't go there.

"Her phone might be flat. We've been out all day, and she Instagrammed a ton of shit for her billions of followers. And you know what the signal is like on the subway."

True.

I open the fridge and flick the top of a Peroni, chugging the entire bottle.

Get your shit together, Jarett.

"Okay, I'll give her an hour and try again."

Kassidy is likely exhausted after last night, and on top of that, a day of shopping with my sister. I don't want her too exhausted for what I have planned tonight.

I tap out a quick text.

> ***Me:*** *Can't wait to see you tonight.*
> ***Me:*** *Get some rest, I have a big night planned.*
> ***Me:*** *Call me when you get this.*

Okay, so three messages. On my second beer, I

find myself wandering around my apartment, unsure what to do next. I'm so eager to see Kassidy, I can't think straight. At least if I were to hear from her, I'd know she's okay.

Time is running out, and I haven't laid eyes on her or kissed her beautiful lips since she left this morning.

An hour later, I wade through my art box to discover my favorite pencils and prepare an easel in the art room. A room I haven't stepped foot in since the accident.

Creativity has eluded me, and fear has overwhelmed me for too long now.

Memories. I dreaded the flood of memories sketching would bring to the forefront of my mind. Ignorance is bliss. I have kept the door to this room locked shut *until now.*

Anxiety threatens to engulf me. Between the concern of not hearing from Kassidy, the thrill of seeing her again soon, and anticipating how much fun we'll have tonight, it's all too much to bear. The need to do something to keep me from going insane is growing stronger by the second.

Before too long, I'm staring at an outlined sketch of Kassidy in front of me.

I let it happen.

It's time.

And I don't feel any guilt for doing so. Memories of the past of Helena and the many times I sketched her, crash over me in waves several times.

Instead of crippling me with pain like the past year, the memories of her inspire me. Music fills my workspace, and I allow hope and lust to fuel my creativity. Kassidy is coming to life in front of me.

I have never sketched any other woman before.

Only Helena.

Never have I sketched without a live subject or photo. This is completely freehand, from memory only.

I recreate the scene from yesterday morning. After our night of passion, I waltz into the bedroom with a cup of coffee to find Kassidy with the sheets tangled around her legs and her long blonde waves spilled over the royal blue pillowcases. She was the picture of pure bliss. Her breast peeked out from the sheet as she stretched her arms above her. With her back arched like a feline, a sleepy grin crept over her face until she was all smiles. Her eyes popped when I moved in to kiss her good morning.

She's so fucking beautiful. Without realizing it, she is reinventing me. One piece at a time, she is putting together the remnants of my shattered heart.

Once again, I believe.

In life.

In hope.

In love.

Reality slams into me, knocking the wind from

my chest.

Love.

I can't love her. She isn't mine to love.

She never will be.

Kassidy has a one-way ticket home to Australia, and there's not a damn thing I can do about it.

One thing I'll forever be grateful for is her presence in my life. If only for five short days, Kassidy has lit my world on fire in the best way.

In less than a week. How is that even possible?

When she leaves, I honestly believe my life will be better because of the five nights I've spent with her.

Stepping away from the portrait, my heart swells.

With pride.

My first masterpiece. I can't wait to show Kassidy.

Speaking of her, the sun has set, and darkness is creeping in and there's still no response. Opening another beer, I ponder my next move.

Deciding not to message or call her in case she's sleeping off the day, I shower and prepare for the evening.

The surprise I have planned for Kassidy tonight is something she'll never anticipate. I hope the bold plans don't backfire on me. It's possibly something I should've run past her first but, I have no expectations for how the night will go. She'll have complete control over what does and doesn't happen.

There's no way I'll let our night be ruined because of a bad judgment call. Maybe I should talk to her on the way. If she's dead against it, I'll abort the mission.

I make a call. "Boss, it's Jarett."

Boss is his nickname, the only name he's known by in the community.

"Hey, man, what can I do for you? Coming in tonight?" he asks.

"Ah, yeah. Two of us."

Dead silence falls between us.

"You bringing a buddy to enjoy the show?"

I laugh. He's never seen me with a woman at the club or otherwise.

"A female friend, yes. Kassidy. She's visiting from Australia."

"Shit, good on you, man. Need me to book a room?"

"Tentatively, yes. I'm not sure how perceptive she is yet."

"Jarett, my man, don't bring any freak show to my club. She better be open to this and know the deal before you both arrive."

"All over it," I confirm.

"See you tonight."

Chapter 13

KASSIDY

Wine nurtures my body while I FaceTime with Raven.

I hate the idea of leaving London.

Leaving Jarett.

And Sophia.

"Don't overthink it, girl," she tells me when I repeat my conversation with Sophia today.

"I'm trying not to, but I don't want to be the cause of a setback for him."

"Does he want this to be more than a fling?"

Honestly, I don't know.

"I doubt it."

I roll over and prop the phone against the pillow.

"I mean, we had a random lunch, and I told him I was here for five nights. Why would he expect more?"

"Expect, no. But hope is a powerful emotion. Be careful he's not holding onto something he shouldn't if you're not interested."

I sigh. My brain hurts.

My heart beats out of sync with my head.

"If I were staying in London, I'd be all for seeing where this went with him. Also, I doubt if the past few days would've played out like it this if I were living here or staying for a decent period."

"All I'm saying is he might be thinking along the same lines."

"But he's married, or was." I huff, feeling like a selfish bitch.

"Kassidy, nothing has changed. It's a few nights. Enjoy them and try to forget what Sophia told you."

Easier said than done.

"I want to forget, I do. What if this is his first fling or sexual encounter since his wife? What if that's the only reason I appeal to him at all? An easy no-strings fling he can forget about because I'm leaving soon."

Shit.

I repeat the words in my head and cover my face.

"Ah fuck, you like him?"

I hold my tongue, ignoring her real question. "Of course, I like him. Sophia, too, but—"

"No, Kass, I mean, you fucking *like* him. Are you sure you're not projecting your feelings onto this situation? It's the Kassidy way to overthink this shit, self-destruct and bail before the poor bastard has a chance to catch up."

I roll away from the screen, sulking. "Don't hold back," I respond dryly.

"The simple truth is this... you have three nights left. Either blow off the guy you enjoy hanging out with and spend the night alone on one of your five nights away or flick him and go out and do your thang."

I hate when she's right.

It's not a complicated situation. I've let my feelings, whatever they are, get in the way.

"You're one hundred percent right as fucking always. I'll head out tonight and do my *thang*. Tomorrow, Jarett will be a thing of the past."

If I say it often enough, I will eventually believe it.

"Fuck lust. I need pure unadulterated chemistry and some hard-core sex."

"Aaanddd... she's back!" she wails through the phone.

We say our goodbyes because it's the wee hours of the morning in Australia, and I'm lucky she woke up to my call.

A Few Hours Later...

Peeling my eyes open, I rise from the bed slightly disorientated. The last thing I recall is Jarett texting, and then I must have drifted off to sleep.

My body screams at me, my feet angry at me for walking the city in heels today. I plug my phone in to charge, silence it, and run the tub. I cram myself like a sardine into the doll-sized bath with the bottle of wine I grabbed on my way back this afternoon.

It's getting dark out as I submerge my top half in the hot soapy water with my thighs and feet dangling over the edge. What a fucking sight if someone were to walk in right now. I laugh as I sip from the bottle.

My muscles relax into the heat, and I swoosh around to change position so my poor feet can soak up the pleasures. I drain a little water out and refill with warmer water, pulling my knees to my chest and stretching my feet to rest against the wall.

Heavenly bliss.

Sweat pools on my forehead, and I tie my hair on top of my head in a messy bun. The wine turns from crisp and refreshing to warm and scintillating, flooding my body with an alcohol-filled hum.

Yeah, this is life. I deserve this. Enjoying the ambiance, I allow my eyes to drift shut. I picture candles burning around the outskirts of the tub, soft music playing in the background, and the aroma of salted caramel seeping into my space.

A knock at the door startles me, causing me to almost drop my wine, my liquid courage for the night. My pre-drinks with me, myself, and I.

I still in the cooling water, clutching the bottle to my chest, and listen as the knocking continues.

My eyes spring a leak when I hear Jarett's voice. "Kassidy, answer the door."

I want to see him. I do. But I don't trust myself.

He doesn't deserve pity or awkward interactions because he's lost his wife. I wish I could rewind the day and alter the course of the conversation.

"Kassidy, I'm worried. Please, call me!"

Feeling like a mega-bitch, I stay in the tub for about an hour after, paranoid Jarett is hovering at the door, waiting for some sign of life.

My phone pings a dozen times, each time increasing my anxiety.

Attempting to stand, my brain is foggy, my skin shriveled and prune-like.

I make my way to my phone and find a message from Chloe.

> **Chloe:** *Raven filled me in. Go get it tonight, girl. Can't wait to see you in a few days!*

Ashamed of myself for avoiding Jarett and angry at myself for being such a weak-minded selfish bitch, I confess my sins in response to Chloe's message.

> **Chloe**: *Suck it up, princess, it's your vay-cay. I want to know what the club is like! What club?*

I sit on the edge of the sofa and scroll through the messages. Most of them are from Jarett, but there's one from Raven.

> **Raven:** *Kass, you must go for me! BDSM club close to you, single ladies free. Get slut-dressed and have fun for both of us.*

I click on the link she included.

Falling onto the sofa, I scroll through the pages of their website. It promises classy, discreet fun. A members-only club opening to singles once a month. The sex gods are on my side because tonight is singles night.

Safety guaranteed, sexy attire required, and no requirements to join in. Watching only is allowed. My libido stirs, and I consider what to wear.

Visiting a sex club is something I've often discussed with Raven. More specifically, an underground London cellar like I read about in Raven's smut books she shares with me.

Tonight, I'll discover if there's any truth or accuracy to these clubs.

I'm red hot with anticipation just thinking about it.

I don't have to engage in any sexual acts. I'll treat it as an assignment and report to Raven. I'm not vanilla, but I've also never considered being suspended and whipped or fucked in front of a room full of strangers.

I'm a caramel swirl.

My clit throbs at the memory of Jarett spanking my ass. The harder his hand fell over my cheeks, the more I moved around his cock. The pain heightened my pleasure in a way it never had before.

This club might be exactly what I need tonight to take my mind off Jarett. I'd be so hot and wonton afterward, I'll have to go clubbing and find me a man to bring home.

Thirty minutes later, I'm stepping once again into my heeled boots. These babies will be the death of me, but they're the warmest footwear I have with me.

I guide them over my crotchless fishnets running beneath my leather skirt. If I had a kink, it would be wearing fishnets. I love the texture against my skin and wear them often beneath tights and jeans. It's almost as weird as my fascination with collecting scarves.

Laughing, I imagine my tombstone when I die.

Caramel swirl, fishnet-wearing scarf collector.

I finish my look with a thick lacy corset and long satin jacket, then fix my makeup. I shoot off a quick text to Jarett and grab my coat.

Kassidy: *Sorry to make you worry, I'm fine. Maxed out, going to sleep it off tonight. Talk tomorrow.*

Short and sweet.

"No cell phones allowed," the bouncer warns, retrieving my phone and adding it to the packet with my details attached.

One foot after the other, I move confidently toward the man and woman at the next door. My shoulders back, chin lifted, my jittery nerves fall by the wayside.

"Hello, miss, may I take your coat?"

"Thank you, yes." The woman takes the packet containing my phone, and I remove my coat to hand to the statue-like gentleman who's skillfully keeping his eyes on everything around him but attending to my needs at the same time.

I pull my satin jacket tighter around me and ensure the wrap is secured firmly. I didn't have the lady balls to walk around in my corset until I knew what was waiting for me on the other side of the door.

"Are you meeting with anyone, ma'am?" the older man asks me.

"No. It's my first time here. I'm only visiting London for a few days."

He nods silently, and his eyes dart to the woman who was looking me up and down.

"I suspect you may want to remove that layer as well," she says, and I hesitate. "Trust me," she continues and waits patiently for my reaction. Reluctantly, I peel off the extra layer to reveal my lace corset I picked up at the vintage boutique store today. My boobs pop from the top, showing my deep cleavage, and I feel proud of my girls.

I can do this.

My blonde waves fall heavily to where the low-cut corset gathers high above my ass. With a little torso showing, my naval bar is on full display.

The doors open, and I'm given two free drink vouchers and directed toward the bar. My steps are slow as my eyes dart left and right, unsure where to look and what to take in first. There are people spread everywhere. Some stand alone at the bar, people-watching, while others dance seductively on the dance floor.

Couples drape themselves over the sofa and enjoy making out in front of an audience. In the corner at the other side of the bar, a woman dressed only in heels, a lace corset, and a studded collar is suspended to a wooden cross, being teased by a man. I observe her eyes roll back in her head, and her body quiver beneath his touch as he caresses her with his mouth.

Then she yelps.

Did he bite her?

I make my way to the bar, the laser lighting and seductive music enhancing the thrill from my earlier wine binge. I stand between two unoccupied stools, debating whether to perch myself on a chair and risk revealing everything under my short skirt.

"What can I get you?"

The woman behind the bar lacks personality but makes up for it with her luscious curves. It's difficult to see her true beauty under the weight of her makeup, but with her jet-black curls pulled back in a tight ponytail high on her head, her high cheekbones and sharp features give her the perfectly put-together mistress look

"Margarita on the rocks, please." I hand her one of my drink vouchers, and she accepts it with a smile.

Dressed in a scantily clad leather brasier with matching booty shorts and knee-high boots, I couldn't help but peer over the bar at her while she makes my drink.

I observe those surrounding me at the bar and notice I'm the only woman standing here. When my margarita is served, I'm unsure whether to sit at the bar with the men who are watching me with hawk-eyes ready to pounce and make me their next meal or find a seat alone to take in the atmosphere. Across the way, I scope out a small table and single armchair facing the majority of the action in the room.

Taking a sip of my margarita, I appreciate the tang of the tequila and lime on my lips until I begin to feel too much like prey.

I shift uncomfortably, moving the weight off my stance from one foot to the other. As I'm about to move to the single chair, the woman behind the bar approaches me again.

"This your first time here?" she asks while wiping the bar.

"That obvious, huh?"

Her eyes shift between the guy at the end of the bar and me. "Looks like you have an admirer," she whispers subtly, pointing her head in his direction.

"Oh," I offer awkwardly, glancing in the general direction. "I'm only here as a favor to a friend, just checking things out."

"Sing out if you need anything. My name is Tessa, by the way."

"Kassidy, nice to meet you."

Another one of the guys calls to her, so I use the opportunity to flee.

Eclectic music filters through the sound system,

and I take a seat in the plush armchair, crossing my legs and ready to watch others play.

There's a couple between the woman dancing in the suspended cage and the couple whipping a woman tied to the cross. It appears he's guiding her pleasure. Gently removing the shy and apprehensive part of her, the pleasure is transforming her right in front of my eyes, and I can't look away. I can sense her letting go, enjoying the moment at the mercy of this man.

After a few minutes of observing them, I lean forward to pick up my margarita. Mindlessly, I swirl the straw around the ice cubes and scan the club. A sign hanging above a darkened hallway catches my eye.

'Private Rooms.'

I wonder if there are rooms with a private viewing area.

While I didn't come here to participate, I can't deny how turned on I am after watching the couples in this room.

I'm here to soak up the environment, take mental notes, and report back to Raven. Above all things, I need to shift my wandering mind away from Jarett. I gave myself one hour to scope out this kink club when I arrived before I plan to disappear upstairs to the nightclub in search of a suitor for a few hours of fun.

Any man who isn't Jarett.

People begin to gather at the opposite side of the bar. Intrigued, I gravitate toward them. Men and women of all shapes and dress codes stand in a tight-knit circle. I elbow my way into the small crowd until I can see the center attraction.

A woman is kneeling on a shaggy rug, her hands tied behind her back with two men standing directly in front of her—completely naked—their cocks erect and glistening beneath the fluorescent purple light above.

My chest expands to stabilize the anxious beating of my heart.

As I watch one of the men blindfold her, envy overpowers me. I can't take my eyes off the trio.

The men peruse the crowd as if to ensure their audience is ready. Invested in the pleasure they are about to derive from this woman, they move closer to her. Their cocks gently slap her cheeks until her mouth opens and her tongue protrudes, desperate for contact with them.

One of the men slaps himself on her tongue repetitively until her tongue begins to swirl, and her lips close around him.

Standing proudly, hands on his hips, the man begins to flex his hips, moving his cock in and out of her mouth. A slow and steady rhythm. The second man's eyes are glued to the woman worshiping his friend while he strokes himself fluidly.

I'm so fucking turned on I can barely think straight.

When the man pulls out, he signals for his friend to step in to replace him. He also teases her lips as she licks at his precum. My mouth falls open slightly as the first guy moves behind the woman, stands over her legs, and places his hand around the front of her throat.

He whispers something in her ear as he holds her throat and strokes himself with perfect rhythm. She nods.

My head rocks, agreeing with her.

I want to be her.

Snapping out of my trance, I consciously become aware of the couples playing with each other or themselves, as they too watch the trio.

My eyes lift across the circle, and my breath stalls in my chest.

Dark, angry eyes connect with mine, and my flushed skin burns beneath his stare.

Jarett.

How the fuck did he know where I was?

A wall of people blocks my fall as I stumble backward, desperate to escape his glare. Turning, I push through the crowd.

I lied to him.

To protect him from falling for me.

No, to protect *my heart* from breaking when I leave.

OMG, what have I done?

What must he think of me for being here?

For telling him I was exhausted and staying in for the night?

My heart beats unevenly against my chest wall, so hard the vibrations spread through to my throat. Butterflies swoop viciously from side to side in the pit of my stomach. As my throat begins to tighten and the room closes in around me, I pull a melting cube of ice from my drink and slip it into my mouth.

Breaking free from the crowd, I take a second to find my bearings and seek out the exit.

Tessa, the woman from the bar, approaches me with a concerned look on her face. "Kassidy, is everything okay?"

I look behind me for the first time, and not surprisingly, Jarett is right there.

And his wild and crazy eyes are focused only on me.

Chapter 14

JARETT

What the actual fuck is she doing here?

Did she know I was planning to bring her here tonight?

No way, it's impossible.

Pushing through the crowd, I make my way to Kassidy, who's speaking with Tessa, a woman I only know from coming here, but she has listened to me pour my heart out over a few whiskeys more than once.

My eyes connect with Kassidy as she glances back at me, and I don't like what I see. Her gaze is filled with sadness, and my heart plummets to the floor.

Kassidy escapes down the hall as I quickly explain myself to Tessa, who waits for me to catch up. Her arms are folded tight across her chest, and she wears a stern expression which screams, *'you'll have to go through me to get to her.'*

Sympathetically, she touches my arm and nods to where Kassidy has disappeared. On fast legs, I rush down the hall just in time to catch a glimpse of her walking into a viewing room.

The fuck?

Without thinking, I barge into the small room and instantly wish I hadn't. An older guy sits at one end of the row of chairs, tucking himself back into his pants before he politely and shamelessly excuses himself from the room.

Leaving us alone.

After fixing the sign on the door to show it's occupied, I glare at Kassidy. Her eyes are transfixed on the couple in the adjacent room as if I hadn't just barged in on her sitting near a guy flogging his dick in front of her.

"Seriously, Kassidy?" I implode. Her head whips to me, but her eyes don't meet mine. "You lie to me about being too tired and needing to stay in bed, then show up at a fucking sex club and hide out with a stranger while he jerks off to this?" My arms fly out in the direction of the woman gagged, blindfolded, and tied up while getting whipped in the next room.

"This?" she blurts out, pointing at the couple. "Isn't this the same as what we were both just watching outside? And that poor bastard probably wasn't happy that I barged in here to get away from you either."

"Why did you lie?" I ask through gritted teeth.

My ego hurt, admittedly, but this unsettled feeling isn't a result of a bruised ego. It stems from a world of hurt caused by a lying woman.

My wife.

Emotions I never expected to feel again wash over me as I glare at Kassidy, only an arm's length away.

"Why did you?" she snaps, tears lining her eyes.

Her response flattens me. "I never lied to you, sweetheart. You never asked me if I was married, and I never mentioned it because technically, I'm fucking not. My wife is dead."

The words fly out of my mouth before I can sensor them, and I fall to the chair at my side, my face in my hands.

"Jarett, fuck," Kassidy whispered. "How did you know that's what I was talking about?"

I sigh miserably. "When I called Sophia a second time concerned about you, she mentioned your conversation at lunch today. I just assumed."

"I'm sorry, I didn't know how to act once I found out."

"How to act?" I look up at her and lounge back in the chair. She plops into the seat beside me. "Does the fact I had a wife who's now gone change anything between us? For fuck's sake, you'll be back on a flight to Australia in a few days, anyway."

"Exactly, Jarett. A fling with a chick who's visiting your city for a few days may seem like the best way to get back on the horse, so to speak, but I'm not sure I'm comfortable being that woman."

Kassidy stands, she's ready to leave.

I grab her hand. "Please, Kassidy. Can we talk about this?"

She looks over her shoulder to the room next door where the guy is now fucking his partner. "Think we can talk someplace else?"

I nod, and a few minutes later, we walk out of the club in search of some place quiet to have a conversation I never thought I'd be having.

"I like you. Fuck, I respect you, Kassidy. This isn't some dirty fling where I hope never-to-speak-to-you-once-you-leave kind of situation. Not for me, anyway." I silently plead with her to give me a chance.

In a quiet twenty-four-hour coffee shop a few doors up from Kassidy's hotel, we sit in a booth, unable to look at each other.

"I'm sorry I lied to you about staying in," Kassidy whispers. "I wasn't sure how to handle the news about Helena, and I needed time to think."

I nod silently. "Why did it bother you so much?"

She contemplates this for a few moments. "Honestly, I don't know. My heart hurt for you when Sophia told me. She mentioned you hadn't really seen anybody since and... well, I'm leaving soon, and I didn't want that to be a thing, I guess."

"You were concerned I'd be broken by you leaving? Or is this your way of creating distance between us, so you don't get hurt when you leave?"

Does Kassidy have feelings for me?

"Don't be a grade-A pompous jerk. I didn't mean it like that. We don't need to be having these sorts of conversations just because we have spent a few great nights together. Why not leave it as it is and go our separate ways now?"

I frown into my coffee. "That's what you want? To walk away and forget this happened?" I glance at her, where she sits picking at the label on her latte.

"I never said I wanted to forget. But leaving is inevitable. Why draw it out longer than necessary when it means you now feel the need to explain your tragic past?"

The tragic past that's faded into the background of my life since meeting Kassidy. Yeah, right.

"Here's what I know, sweetheart," I offer, leaning forward. "I don't feel the need to explain shit about me or my life. Everything I have told you is because I feel so fucking comfortable with you. I never spoke of Helena because I've never really spoken to anyone about her, and I didn't want to bring down *your* mood. You're on holiday, remember?"

Kassidy smiles weakly, and her eyes glisten.

"As I said, when you leave, I hope we can stay in touch. Who knows, life may have a way of us seeing each other again one day. Either way, I know Helena is a part of my life I'd discuss with you when I was ready. And honestly, you're the one I'll want to discuss her with out of all the people I know. There's something about you... I can't put my finger on it, and I don't understand it, but I believe you entered my life at this time for a specific reason."

I take a breath and sit back. "There, I said it. I only hope that doesn't freak you out."

Word vomit at its finest. Why can't I speak like I think? In drips and drabs.

"I'm sorry, Jarett." She places her hand on mine from across the table, and I capture her fingers in mine. "I'm not pressuring you to talk about her. I don't need to know anything at all. And who the fuck am I to feel even the slightest bit used when I'm openly using you as my tour guide, travel companion, drinking buddy, dance partner, and after-dark sex pal?"

"Ouch." I clutch my chest and make stabbing actions with my hands. We both laugh, and it's about fucking time. "You know how to knock a guy when he's down, huh?"

She smiles sadly, and for the first time, I'm unable to get a clear reading of her thoughts. There's a distance between us which wasn't there before. Even when we first laid eyes on each other, there was something familiar and warm that has since dissipated.

"I'm really tired. Can we maybe meet for coffee or breakfast tomorrow?"

My heart sinks. Kassidy isn't planning on us spending tonight together. For all I know, last night could've been our last.

"Sure," I reply, forcing out the biggest smile I can muster the energy for.

"I'd love you to come by the gallery if you can. I have something I wanted to show you tonight before we went out."

"Of course, I'm sorry the night didn't plan out as it should have."

"Me, too." I sigh, getting ready to leave.

"Where had you planned for us to go anyway?" she asks as we step outside.

I laugh. How fucking ironic.

"You wouldn't believe me if I told you," I joke.

And she didn't, at first.

Feeling more comfortable about the evening's events after she told me how she had come to be at the club, I share something with her that I've never mentioned to anybody.

"My history with the club itself is short, though I've always been interested in, what would you say, light bondage? Since Helena, the club has been my escape… a safe place to get out of my head and keep me from falling into the arms of a woman who could break my heart again."

The pity in her eyes isn't something I want to see and probably why I avoid talking about Helena or my grief at all.

I pull her close and kiss her cheek.

"Until you came along, that is," I whisper into her hair.

I'm unsure if she heard me, but I don't care. It's the truth.

I watch Kassidy walk away, following her until she turns into her hotel building. Knowing she's safe, I saunter off in the opposite direction.

Alone.

And missing her already.

Maybe she was right.

Why prolong the inevitable?

Chapter 15

KASSIDY

When I wake, it's much later than usual, and my mind is on the woman and the two men in the club last night. I consider staying in bed a little longer and giving my bullet vibe a workout until I remember the hurt on Jarett's face as I tried *badly* to explain why I'd ditched our date.

I was and still am confused.

Sighing, I roll out of bed with a thud as my feet hit the floor. I can't allow emotions to ruin one of only five days in London.

Despite my lackluster mood, I torture myself with a lukewarm shower, step into a pair of tights and cover them with an oversized sweatshirt. Paired with thick woolly socks with padding on the souls for additional comfort, I zip up my boots and grab my coat.

All in under ten minutes.

Yeah, I'm starving and risk turning into a foul-tempered tyrant if I'm not fed. Too much wine and tequila the night before will do that to a girl. There's a little street cart by the river that sells the most delicious-looking oversized Nutella crepes, and based on the grumbling deep in the pit of my stomach as I pictured the gooey sweetness, that's what I'm having for brunch.

Topped with whipped cream, strawberries, and hot Nutella sauce, I sit on the sidewalk and people watch while I consume it. I all but eat the plate and order a chai latte with a triple shot of caffeine from the canteen on the corner to polish off the unhealthiest yet to-die-for breakfast I've ever eaten.

Enjoying my latte, I tap out a quick message to Jarett with a photo of my breakfast ensemble which I managed to take before scarfing it down. It only takes a few seconds for him to reply.

Jarett: *Where are you? I just got to the gallery.*

His second text reads...

Jarett: *That looks incredibly naughty in the best way.*

Believe me, I want to be all kinds of naughty after

last night. When I returned to my room after leaving Jarett, I called Raven to fill her in. To say she was hideously jealous was an understatement. We agreed to go to a club together when I return home, and she knows just the one to visit.

Since I left, she found out that Sean, the guy she's seeing, secretly owns a club in Brisbane. Well, he's a silent partner, but his cousin, Gina, runs it, and we can go anytime.

We also add a London club experience to our bucket list for the following year. I'd love to experience this city with my besties.

I'm still thinking about the conversation with Raven about cutting ties with Jarett when my phone buzzes again on the table.

Jarett: *I can come to you if you'd prefer?*

I shouldn't want to see him as badly as I do. Could he be right when he suggested I want to create the distance before *I* get too attached?

I respond with my location, and my phone lights up again.

Jarett: *On my way.*

The problem isn't my need for distance, it's the strong connection I have with Jarett and my increasing anxiety surrounding my flight home on

Monday morning.

I'm torn between seeing my girls back home, getting back to reality, and concentrating on my career progression or staying in London on a permanent fucking holiday with the greatest guy I've ever met.

I'm pathetic.

A silhouette of the woman I was when I arrived.

Fairy tale endings, my ass.

"Who's an ass and what fairy tale?"

I jump at the sound of his voice beside me. Geez, I must have been talking to myself. Please sky, open and suck me into oblivion.

"Huh?" Like the raving lunatic I am, I pretend I'm none the wiser.

Jarett chuckles and hands me a giant-sized cup of coffee. "I know you love to have a week's worth of coffee to start your mornings, so I didn't hesitate in getting the largest takeout cup I could find on my walk here. Plus, talking to yourself at..." he glances at his watch and raises his eyebrows in pretend shock, "... nine fifteen on a Saturday morning deserves the strongest caffeine available."

"Funny." I roll my eyes, smiling up at him and thank him for the coffee.

He takes a seat beside me, so we're both looking out over the River toward Westminster. "So, what do you have against fairy tales, Kassidy? Do tell," he prompts me for my darkest secrets.

Not really, but you get the idea. I don't fancy saying the words out loud.

"Honestly, I can't remember what I was thinking now."

Jarett accepts my answer without question as he watches a boat glide past us. "Okay, so let's talk about today, then. What do you have in mind for day four in London?"

Another thing I haven't given any thought to.

Have I become so reliant on him these past few days having him as my tour guide that I've forgotten to think for myself?

"Well," I pause, and he waits, anticipating my grand idea.

Shaking my head, I laugh. "Nothing. I'm drawing a blank. My feet are exhausted, my brain is tired, and…" I pause, my laughter disappearing. "And I sincerely apologize for yesterday and last night. I think you may have been right. I'm deflecting as much if not more for my benefit."

Saying it out loud takes a weight off my shoulders I didn't know until now that I've been carrying. No wonder my feet are so fucking sore.

Jarett places his hand on my thigh and gives it a gentle squeeze. "No need to apologize. Let's put it behind us. Our time is limited, and despite the creative thoughts you had about me, I like you, Kassidy, and I want to get to know you more before you leave."

His words make my heart happy, and a genuine smile creeps over my face.

"I'd like that. Very much."

"Thank fuck!" He lets out in a gush as if he's been holding his breath. Leaning forward, he reaches inside his coat pocket and pulls out some tickets. "I may have taken it upon myself to plan our day. You know, hoping you'd come to your senses and not deny me your time."

Taking the brochures from him, I plant a chaste kiss on his lips. There's a tour bus heading out in an hour to visit Cotswold, Stonehenge with the promise of glorious scenery, tasty foods, and guided tours. A day of history lessons and scouring old castles and historical landmarks.

"A day in the country sounds like heaven, especially with the beautiful weather." I raise my hands to the sky, emphasizing the beauty of the clear skies and sunshine raining down on us. It was a nice change from the drizzling rain, reckless winds, and blankets of snow I had experienced so far.

"Agreed. But first, I need you to accompany me back to the gallery as I have a surprise waiting for you that I'm both excited and nervous as fuck to show you." He stands and offers me his hand.

All the confusion I woke with this morning vanishes as we walk in silence, hand in hand.

The butterflies in my stomach are probably

drunk on Nutella, but I know it's more than that. Being in Jarett's presence invigorates me.

Balances me.

The man he is makes me want more.

More of him.

More from life.

More for my future.

Excitement bubbles within, and the desires of the heart aren't far behind. But neither of these are aligned with my professional goals.

"Close your eyes, love."

I think we're standing outside his office. He didn't bring me to this section of the gallery on my first visit. Without hesitating, I close my eyes and trust him to guide me safely.

The door opens, and after a few steps forward, the door latches behind us.

"Not yet," he says, dropping my hand and taking me by the shoulders from behind.

"Is this a kinky ploy, sir?" I tease.

He responds with a soft chuckle in my ear. "You'd like that, wouldn't you, dirty girl?"

Goosebumps spread over my delicate skin as his warm breath whispers over my bare neck.

My body hums with anticipation. We stop shuffling forward, and he moves to my side.

"Before you open your eyes, what you're about to see is something extremely personal I want to show you. But it's not the surprise I have for you."

"Okay." My interest piques to the max.

My palm in his starts to perspire and becomes clammy with my nerves.

"Open your eyes, Kassidy."

Blinking a few times until my eyes adjust to the light, I'm drawn to the large painting on the wall in front of me. I notice Jarett in my side vision, watching me intently, waiting for my reaction.

I'm staring at a bold and gracefully appealing portrait. The same gorgeous woman in all the photos in his section of the gallery downstairs. The woman I referred to as a model he may have worked with.

"Wow," I whisper.

The painting is elegant and eccentric all in one. He captures the natural grace of the woman and encompasses her in a mystical aura. A modern piece of art with a timeless centerpiece. *The woman.*

My mouth hangs open in awe of his artistic talent. I turn to him, his eyes still focused intently on me, waiting patiently for a response.

"Jarett, I have no words. This portrait is magnificently beautiful. And the woman, her elegance…" my words fade out, his expression remains unchanged, and he offers nothing further. He simply waits.

"Is this woman your… wife?" I whisper, unable to think of any other reason this piece would be so personal to him.

"Yes, this is…" he turns to the portrait, "… was, Helena." He smiles wistfully as he returns his attention to me.

"She's incredibly beautiful," I tell him. The words are not nearly strong enough to do her justice.

"Helena was many things," he begins. "Beautiful was definitely one of them." He guides me to the sofa across the room. A room divider is pulled across the area, and I wonder what lies on the other side.

"You asked the other day about the woman in the portraits downstairs. I should've told you about her then."

Oh, Jarett.

I hate that my reaction to the situation led him to feel this way.

Taking his hand in mine, I rub my thumb over his knuckles and look him in the eye. "This part of your life is never anything you should feel compelled to discuss if you're not ready. And it wasn't the time nor place to divulge such painful memories. I completely understand you not saying anything. Honestly, I wish Sophia hadn't mentioned it because of the rift I've allowed it to cause between us."

Silently, he pulls me to him in a comforting embrace and kisses my neck tenderly below my ear. "Thank you," he whispers.

I want to remind him this is only a fling, and personal details are unnecessary. If he were married and his wife still alive, then yes, that's information I would've been furious if he hadn't shared with me. But this is different.

Pulling back from the intimate hug, he starts to speak openly about Helena. "She was the love of my life, I thought. The night before her modeling contract began in New York, I intercepted a text from the male model she was contracted to work with. They had worked together on past projects. She traveled a lot, and while I could've gone with her many times, I always opted to stay and focus on building my empire here." He shifts uncomfortably in his seat, his eyes drawn to the floor.

I wait for him to continue, sensing he needs to have this discussion more for himself than to fill me in. And I'm happy to listen.

"The text was about *'their'* room, Oliver telling her how much he couldn't wait to have her in his arms again." He sighs, avoiding my gaze.

My heart breaks for the man sitting in front of me. Not only did he have to deal with the sudden death of his wife, but she died soon after her lies and deceit were exposed. Cheating isn't an issue to be dealt with in one evening, and she left the following day.

"Naturally, I scanned through the previous messages, and it appeared that she had been planning to leave me, or at least that's what she had been telling Oliver."

"Oh my God, Jarett, I'm so sorry. I don't know what to say." I move back into the sofa and prop my leg beneath me.

He shakes his head. "Words can't change anything. Even at that point, nothing she said to me would change a thing. Funnily enough, when I confronted her about it, she barely batted an eyelid. As if sleeping around was part of who we were."

Finally, he raises his eyes to me. "I was gutted. I couldn't have imagined being with any other woman, let alone living as if it weren't happening. It's probably a downfall for me, but I'm all or nothing. Even this kind of thing..." he waves his finger back and forth between us, "... I never dreamed of having a fling or one-night stand with a woman, even before I was married."

My heart skips a beat or two, and not for the reasons you might think.

As much as I try to hide it, my face falls. Quickly,

my gaze darts around the room while I collect myself.

"Don't go there, love." Jarett takes my chin gently between his fingers and guides my head up until my eyes lock with his. "I've never thought wrong of it, it just wasn't for me. I want that spark, a connection if you will, but something more than sexual. And that's exactly what I felt the moment I laid eyes on you."

I force a smile, but the worry remains. I see it echoed back at me through Jarett's gaze. He chuckles. "Maybe not the 'moment' I laid eyes on you because if I remember correctly, your head was directly in alignment with the corner of the China cabinet. My first instinct was to grab hold of you."

He runs his fingers through my hair, his touch so soft I melt into it. "Kassidy, the moment I locked eyes with you, a sense of who I was, the old me, began to stir. And each day since we met..." he counts out three days on his fingers for plausible effect, and I laugh softly, "... you've breathed life into me. A man who was nothing short of a soulless shell, and for that, I'll never forget you. Or forgive you for leaving and not staying in touch at least."

A sense of joy crashes over me and calms my soul. The soul that feels very connected to Jarett also. But I'm not yet willing to admit that to him.

Jumping up from the sofa, Jarett holds his hand out to pull me up. "Enough of that sappy shit, we have a bus to catch very shortly. And I still need to share my surprise with you."

He pulls me across the room to where the room divider is latched closed. "First, you should know that every portrait you've seen, in fact, all that I have ever done, have been created with a live subject or from a photograph. I've never been able to or even felt inspired to sketch or paint from memory."

"Okay." I frown, wondering why he's telling me this. He pushes the divider open, and we walk into a large open space. It's filled with color, blank canvases, white sheets, and easels. "Welcome to what I like to call my drawing-room. It's where the magic happens," he states proudly, arms out wide. Over in the corner, he stands by an easel covered in a white sheet cover with splashes of paint.

"Ready?"

"You're killing me... show me. *Please.*"

Ripping off the sheet, he exposes the canvas beneath.

My mouth drops, and my eyes widen with surprise.

It's a black and white sketch of... *me.*

"Oh my God, Jarett. That's me." I clasp my chest with my hand.

"In my bed." He grins cheekily. "You were waking up to me bringing your morning coffee. Your smile was radiant, and the way your wavy hair swept over the pillow, it captivated me."

"You did this from memory?"

"Yes." He kisses the back of my hand. "You're my first."

Swoon.

"Wow, Jarett. I'm... I'm speechless. It's gorgeous, and you're so freaking talented. It's the sweetest surprise I've ever received."

"I haven't been compelled to create art in any form since Helena's accident. Until I thought of you yesterday afternoon—while you were ignoring me—I couldn't put pencil to canvas quickly enough. I simply had to see you, so I sketched you."

He shrugs his shoulders as if this is an everyday skill. One corner of his mouth lifts into a smirk, and I almost say, *fuck the bus tour.*

Jarett is sexy as fuck, and the more I get to know him, the more attractive he is from the inside out. His character and personality are so uplifting despite his fair share of heartache.

I step over and kiss the life out of him.

Our lips meet with vigor.

He moans into my mouth as his hands slip under my sweatshirt and caress my back. I rake my fingers hungrily through his hair as our kiss deepens.

This man. I'm falling headfirst into my childhood fairy tale in a big way.

Chapter 16

KASSIDY

Our day turns out to be the best one yet.

We visit castles, order way too much food from English cottage cafés, and enjoy a picnic on a blanket overlooking the hills and ancient ruins. The weather is glorious, and the company is fucking exceptional.

I met an Aussie couple visiting the area for three months. They were currently trying to get work transfers so they could stay on.

I understand this completely.

I'm falling in love too—with the people, the accents, the food, and the feel of this beautiful city—each minute I spend here, my love grows.

And this countryside.

I imagine many weekends spent visiting the old townships surrounding London if I were able to stay on.

As we exit the bus and say our goodbyes to the other tourists we met and connected with, the tour guide, Anja, stops us. "I hope I'm not being too forward, but I've watched you two today and have to say, you're the most beautiful in love couple I've seen for quite some time."

The world falls away, a cricket ball-sized lump lodges in my throat, and I'm sure the smile I try to force out makes me look like I'm constipated.

"Oh, we're not..." Jarett chuckles, "... no, the two of us, we're just..." he glances at me for help, an astonished expression on his face.

Anja's face morphs into humiliation, and she rushes to apologize. "Forgive me, I'm so sorry. I just assumed. You both look..." her expression softens, "... so much in love."

Jarett puts his arm around my waist and pulls me to him. "Thank you and don't apologize. Sometimes others see things we can't."

Anja gives us a huge smile and retreats with her tail between her legs.

"That wasn't weird at all," I joke, poking Jarett in the ribs as we leave.

His chuckle turns into a full-blown laugh until I'm laughing hysterically too. At what, I'm not sure, but it seems the best way to deal with such an outrageous observation.

One which is clearly incorrect.

Or is it?

As we calm down and a comfortable silence returns, I wonder if Jarett is also reading into Anja's words and how he feels about it.

Me? I am freaking out. I'm not going to lie.

We certainly have chemistry and mutual respect. Yes, I feel something for him but having a stranger believe we're in love? I don't even know what love looks like.

"We should go to the wax museum tomorrow. You interested?" I ask, trying to redirect my thoughts.

"It's a great experience and the perfect place to take lots of fun photos for your Instagram account." He makes a hashtag sign with his fingers. "Kassidy in London," he mocks. That's how I tag all my holiday pics on my account, and he finds it amusing.

I've always been photogenic, and even if I weren't, I wouldn't want to forget any moments I've experienced here, so I guess I have been more snap-happy than usual.

I roll my eyes. "Stalker."

"Hey, it's not stalking if we're friends on Instagram."

I laugh. "No, I guess not."

"I notice none of the photos of us together have been added to your Insta world. You embarrassed to introduce me to your fans?" I glance sideways and stop in my tracks.

"Are you kidding? If I post pics with you, my followers will blow the fuck up in the best way."

His smile reaches his eyes. I take out my phone and pose at his side for a selfie. We shimmy around to get the Big Ben in the background, and I snap a few pics.

"You do know how sexy you are, right? My followers will probably think I have accosted you on the street for a selfie."

"I think you just did."

I slap his chest playfully. "Are you sure about this? You'll forever be famous on my page," I tease, holding the phone up to him, ready to post our collection of silly selfies.

"I'd be honored, Kassidy in London." He brushes a playful peck on my nose and fiddles with my scarf, pulling it tighter around my neck. It's late afternoon, the sky is turning gray, and it's getting colder by the second.

"Looks like it might snow tonight. What should we do?" Jarett asks. We're walking in the direction of my hotel.

"Honestly? I'd love nothing more than to crawl into bed after a hot shower and bottle of wine."

Jarett aims to please and never fails.

We stop for wine and chocolate on our way to my room. While I shower and change into sweats and an oversized jumper, Jarett orders room service. An early dinner and a night of Netflix and chill sound like such a couple thing to do, but I don't care.

We eat at the miniature table in my room, the one Jarett bent me over and fucked me on only days ago. We turn off the lights except for the bathroom to create that romantic atmosphere as we watch the snow fall lightly over Central London.

Perfection.

Afterward, in bed, we share wine and chocolates while we watch a movie on my laptop. As the night progresses, I sink deeper into the mattress and wrap myself tighter in the comforter. My head rests on Jarett's bare chest, my legs entwined with his. And there's where I slept.

Jarett's phone buzzes incessantly on the side table, waking me from my slumber. "Sorry, love." He peels himself away from me. *Did he sleep at all?* I haven't moved a muscle. I wipe my mouth as I sit up, checking for drool as he reaches for his phone and turns off his alarm.

"What on earth do you need an alarm for on a Sunday morning?" Jarett plods back from the bathroom with a cheeky grin on his face. "I'm late for church."

I stare at him, intent on showing no reaction until I can gauge if he's serious or not. "Got your sermon sorted?" I joke.

Jarett laughs and pushes me back onto the bed. Climbing over me, still naked, he kisses me.

Morning breath and all.

I groan, and he pulls back. "What's the matter?"

Bringing my arm to lay across my forehead, I confess. "I'm the worst fling you're ever going to have. A five-night fling should never include a night of Netflix and chill with absolutely no kinky fuckery!"

Jarett shakes his head. "You got it all wrong, sweetheart. You'll be the *only* fling I ever have, and last night was exceptional. I wouldn't change a thing even if I could."

My heart.

Chapter 17

KASSIDY

Day five in London.

My last day.

This time tomorrow, I'll be on my way back to Australia.

A fleeting sadness threatens to overwhelm me.

Jumping out of bed, once again, I'm determined to take this day by the horns and make it my bitch. But I have no idea how to spend the day yet, aside from visiting the wax museum with Jarett.

Standing in the middle of the room with one hand on my hip, my index finger on the other hand repeatedly tapping on my lip, I'm lost in thought when my favorite voice pulls me from my daydream.

"Earth to Kassidy. I said I have to go take care of some business." Jarett sweeps in and kisses me lightly on the cheek.

"So, no church then?" I drop my bottom lip like a petulant child, and my eyebrows draw together. "I was wanting to go with you," I joke.

"I assure you, love, if I were a praying man, I already know what I'd be asking for. But I don't need to step foot inside a church to tell me that." With that, he envelops me in the tightest hug and kisses me lovingly.

For a moment too long.

Now I want to rope him up and throw him back down on the bed and ride him into next week. Instead, I wave him goodbye at the door and agree to meet up with him in the early afternoon. I'm not sure what business he has to deal with on a Sunday, but I guess artists and art dealers work twenty-four seven.

Tomorrow, I fly home and have a full day off after I touch down on Australian soil before I head back to the office on Wednesday. The time off has been more than I dreamed of, though I'm looking forward to getting bogged down in creatives again.

Not so looking forward to saying goodbye to Jarett.

During my last few hours alone in London, I hit the pavement, intent on walking wherever my feet take me—along cobbled lanes, over stone bridges, through narrow lanes, and past shop fronts filled with English bakery goods and greasy chips and vinegar I've grown fond of but are tough on the hips. I wander through small off-street boutiques and bric-a-brac stores until I find myself out front of the cutest little parlor, their shop window filled with antiques and scarves.

Scarves for days.

A childish excitement has me bounding up and down on the spot wondering how much I can fit in my luggage without paying for excess weight charges. Once I walk inside, any thoughts I have about excess luggage go flying out the door.

Scarves and neck warmers hand knitted with thick, soft wool and summery cotton fashion scarves, ones I can wear in Australia, overwhelm me.

Their range extends to leggings of all patterns and colors, gloves, and beanies, not to mention the sarongs and a colorful array of boho-style dresses. I'm in heaven. My love for fabric and intricately woven colors is bred into me by my grandmother. I waltz around the shop silently, sensing Grandma with me as I run the plush delicate materials through my fingers.

It doesn't take long to spend a few hundred dollars and fill a couple of shopping bags. Halfway back to my hotel, my phone starts buzzing. After it rings a few times in a row, I stop and see it's my boss. He's left a voice mail, so I figure I'll wait until I get my purchases safely to my room before I return the call and listen to the message.

To say it was getting on my nerves was an understatement. By the time I walk in the door, I all but want to throw the fucking phone out the window. Setting the bags down, I pull the phone from my coat pocket and find my boss' smiling face on the screen. The latest is a text message saying, 'Call me, it's urgent.'

I should think it urgent if he's called me this many times in such a short period, so I start to panic. *What if there has been an accident or something terrible has happened?*

Malcolm picks up on the first ring. "Thank fuck."

"Everything okay, bossman?"

Mal isn't the type of guy to swear in front of a woman, much less an employee, so his greeting worries me.

"Yes, yes," he answers hastily. "Sorry, Kassidy, for the way I answered and for calling you repeatedly. Everything is okay, but I think you may want to sit down for this."

Okay. What the fuck is going on?

"Is my mother all right?"

"Of course, yes. It's a business-only call, but I am so fu..." he trails off. "I'm excited for us, kid. I had a random call from Gabe Lugreno, Europe's biggest hotelier, an hour ago and called you immediately."

"And he wants a consultant?" I ask, channeling Malcolm's excitement. Consulting a client of that caliber would lift my profile in the industry astronomically.

"Yes and no." Mal continues in a fast fury of words, "They're expanding on some current acquisitions and want to rebrand a few hotels and add a few more to their portfolio. So yes, he wants a consultant to see what we can do, but the work is extensive. He wants a hands-on consultant with fresh and innovative ideas."

I rock back on the bed a little to remove my boots. "And you don't think I can handle such a high-profile campaign?" The words cut like a blunt dagger I don't deserve.

"Kassidy, I believe in you. I always have, you know that. What I'm saying is they want to use a high-profile agency, such as us, and one with Australian influence. They want to Aussie-fy their new hotel brand from the name and logo to the bars and dining areas. And, of course, the structure and décor. So, they don't want an agency *like* us, Kassidy, they want *us.* Period."

"Fucking hell." I'm gobsmacked. This is a huge fucking deal.

"Right? Kiddo, this could make you!"

"When would I have to come back, and for how long?"

A lull in the conversation is one thing, but the silence filtering through the line is daunting.

"That's the kicker," he finally says.

Anxiety kicks in.

Maybe it's hope.

Or the excitement of the unknown.

"All the details, Malcolm. I'm listening."

"When you didn't answer straight away, I panicked. Worried I wouldn't get you in time, so I had to make a call. Lugreno won't be in London for another week, so you could've flown home for a few days and returned, but I thought that was a bit extravagant. So, I've changed your flight."

"You what? Until when?" I screech into the phone, pacing vigorously around my tiny space. I want to open the window and stick my head out in search of fresh air, but I can't.

"I left it hanging in limbo until after the meeting. He's willing to sign us on right now before meeting with you and without an initial consultation."

"How is that possible?" I shriek into the phone. "What if I can't deliver what he needs?" My anxiety levels skyrocket, but freaking out isn't an option. The normally stoic, composed, professional Kassidy is fading quickly. Her arch-nemesis, the overwhelmed, too-good-to-be-true Kassie is slinging her weight around.

"Calm down, Kassie," Mal says, knowing I hate being called Kassie because she's the whiny overwhelming version of me.

Deep breaths.

"You're the perfect person for the job. Pubs and

clubs are you, Kassidy. I tell ya, it's meant to be. And ironically, you're already there. I'd call that fate, wouldn't you?"

No, it makes no sense to me at all.

"How did he know I was here?"

"That's the thing. He didn't. He's been looking around for a while and just recently deciding the Australian influence as the correct approach, he had another hotelier mention us. Don't know who or how but he investigated us. I spoke to the guy for about an hour. He looked over your portfolio online and loved your work. That's when I said you were currently in London."

Plopping onto the sofa with a glass of chilled wine, I sigh. My head is a cloud of half-baked thoughts caught in a windstorm.

"I know you're supposed to check out in the morning, so I'll book you a nice apartment somewhere in the city for the week. Once you meet with Gabe Lugreno, he'll hand over the keys to an apartment in Shoreditch, and it will be all yours, included in your salary. And Kassidy, the package he is offering is indulgent."

Money isn't the issue right now. I trust Malcolm to have my back with that. If it isn't more than I was getting at home, he won't make me stay. "Why the need to move into his apartment, why can't I just stay in the one you book for me?" It's not that I have much stuff to move, I simply don't understand what's expected of me.

"Kassidy, I know this is a lot. And obviously, you can say no, but you and I both know opportunities like this don't come along often, if at all. And as your boss, this is what I have assigned you to do. So, hear me when I say, the apartment in Shoreditch is yours for the length of time you'll be contracted to Gabe Lugreno."

Geez, he's making it sound like this rich bastard is buying me.

"And he's willing to pay you a ten thousand retainer on top of your salary package, you know, for relocation costs, etcetera. You might want some clothes and personal things from home that you couldn't take on a short trip."

My wine spills over as I bolted upright off the sofa. "Relocation? You want me to move here?" My high-pitched screech is an octave or two higher than I knew it could go.

"As I said, in the beginning, he wants a hands-on consultant and the bonus, he doesn't expect you to work alone. He's happy to give you a budget and employ a local team to assist. You'll be overseeing every aspect, so the parts you don't do, you'll be outsourcing and managing the project on his behalf."

The opportunity is exponentially huge. More than anything I've ever dreamed of doing.

Glancing around my tiny space, excitement

rushes through my veins. I'm moving to Shoreditch.

"And how long will I be *contracted* to him as you put it?"

"Initially, it will be a twelve-month contract."

"Initially?"

One whole year in London. Yes, the idea of staying longer had crossed my mind many times over the previous few days, but twelve-fucking-months?

"Of course, you can fly home a few times a year, all expenses paid. Think of it as an extended holiday, Kassidy. And remember, you'll be spending your days in pubs and clubs. This contract was made for you."

Having heard all the information I can endure for the moment, so we end the call. I need a margarita to calm my nerves and wrap my head around this significant change in my plans. I plant my feet back inside my boots and grab my coat, leaving all my purchases from earlier in a pile on the floor.

Where's the nearest bar?

Chapter 18

KASSIDY

"Kassidy! I was hoping I'd find you here."

Sophia is standing at my door ready to knock when I fling it open on my crusade to drink my weight in tequila. She smiles, rushing me for a hug and a friendly kiss.

"Sophia, hi. What are you doing? I was about to head out for a margarita. Join me?"

She claps her hands together with excitement. "Abso-fucking-lutely. My treat."

Ten minutes later, we're sitting at a bar watching a trainee mix our margaritas. It's happy hour, so if he fucks them up, no harm done.

"When I stopped by the gallery on my way over, Jarett showed me the portrait he did of you. It was exquisite." Sophia watches as I run my finger around the edge of my finished glass, collecting all the sugary syrup. Licking the yummy goodness from my fingertips unapologetically, I smile dreamily.

"It's a gorgeous portrait," I agree. "A beautiful and heartfelt surprise," I add, looking at her.

She sits half-swiveled toward me, her arm on the bar and her face resting casually in the palm of her hand. Her eyes are tender and trained intently on me.

"I don't suppose you could extend your vay-cay an extra week or two?"

I'd just taken a sip of my drink and almost choke. Coughing and spluttering, I wipe my mouth with the back of my hand. Class isn't in my corner right now.

Not yet ready to discuss my change of plans, I'm unsure how to answer her. What would my staying in London mean for Jarett and me? A relationship is out of the question. This is a colossal professional opportunity and not one I can afford to ruin by splitting my attention. Besides, Jarett deserves a woman's full attention.

"You okay, Kassidy? You seem a little off," Sophia reflects with a look of concern.

Nodding, I force a smile. "One hundred percent. Now, tell me why I should extend my holiday an extra week?"

Sophia has that same look of excitement on her face as she had when I mentioned margaritas earlier back at my room. "Next Saturday is my fortieth, and I'm overdue for a party. It's going to be epic, and I'd love you to be there."

"Fortieth? No way are you hitting the big four-o. I wouldn't have picked you to be much older than me."

She throws her head back, laughing. "You're the sweetest, but I know you know I'm older than Jarett." She winks. I desperately want to tell her I'll be here, not only for the weekend and her party but for the next twelve months at least.

Except for my girlfriends back home and my mother, I want to tell Jarett first. I need to make some phone calls as soon as possible. Still coming to terms with the change of plans, I picture what life in London will look like if Jarett and I end this façade, this fling.

Part of me acknowledges the risk of allowing a relationship to take over my life. The other part, a loud inner voice, is yelling *this could be fate*.

My real-life fairy tale.

"Where did you go just now?"

Sophia's words break my inner thoughts. "I'm sorry, I was picturing you partying it up and wondering how I could make it happen to be here to celebrate with you." With that, her infectious smile touches my heart. If I stay, I have a true friend in Sophia. Provided my whatever-this-is-or-isn't relationship with her brother doesn't tear our friendship to shreds.

"You would contemplate changing things around and staying for my party?" Her eyes sparkle, and I love that my sticking around makes her so happy.

"I'll see what I can do in the next twelve hours, you never know what life has in store." I squeeze her hand reassuringly.

My bag vibrates. Pulling out my phone, I see Jarett is calling. We're due to meet up soon, and he must be wondering where I am. "Hello, you finished your business meetings?" I greet him.

Out of the corner of my eye, I notice Sophia cock her head to one side, a questioning look on her face. She stopped by to see him on her way here, so I'm guessing he's been free for a little while.

"Wasn't so much a meeting, just several things I had to act on and finalize before tomorrow, but yes, I'm done and all yours. Where are you?"

"Currently drinking half-priced margaritas with your beautiful sister, who apparently, is older than you, though she doesn't look a day over thirty," I tease. Sophia chuckles beside me and cups her face in the palm of her hands, batting her eyelids.

The young bartender catches her doing this, and I'm fairly sure it makes his day.

"Ah, yes, funny, aren't you? Which bar? And you two better not be ganging up on me."

I roll my eyes and chuckle into my phone. "Never." Telling him where to find us, he promises to see us in twenty minutes. For a large city, it seems he's never far from me. Spending most of his waking hours at the gallery and me staying in Central London helps. Moving to Shoreditch will be a different story.

Except Jarett also has an apartment there, not far from Maximum, where I spent my first night. Anxiety spikes, thinking about the what-ifs, but it's not going to help me or anybody else to overanalyze everything.

However, I have to escape this get-together at some point to contemplate the coming months, do some research on my new position and contractor. Most importantly, I need to call home, so the girls know not to expect me on the flight home tomorrow.

So much to do, yet I'm supposed to celebrate my last night in London with Jarett.

"You know the rest of your day is a write-off, right?" Sophia says as I end the call. When I glimpse her blank expression, she continues, "My brother will want you all to himself for your last night here, but as the three of us, Jarett, myself, and Roman usually catch up at Maximum on Sunday nights, I'm going to suggest you join us before he steals you away."

I do love the sound of that. Both a night at the speakeasy and being whisked off to spend alone time with Jarett. Hopefully naked and sweating. It's fitting my first and last night will be enjoyed at the same place surrounded by the same fabulous people.

Only it's no longer my last night, and I'm undecided how I feel about that.

"What a great idea. Count me in." I grin. "Although..." I pause, debating how to plant the seed for some time alone, "... I should make some calls to work and family and see what I can do about changing flights and staying longer." I raise my eyebrows and chew the inside of my lip nervously. I didn't want to lie, but I'm also not ready to give her the whole story just yet.

Sophia's on board. "Yes, you certainly do. I'll help keep Jarett occupied to give you the time you need. I think it would be wise not to say anything to him about this until you know whether it's happening or not."

I'm surprised by her wanting to keep it a secret, but then again, Sophia is super protective of Jarett, so I shouldn't be. Smiling, I raise my glass to her and slurp down the rest of my margarita. Sliding the empty glass toward the center of the bar, I summon the bartender. "Two more, please."

"I don't want Jarett to get his hopes up at the potential extra time with you for it not to happen. I know he'll pretend to be *adultish* about it, but he'll be disappointed."

"No problem," I agree, squeezing her arm lightly

to reassure her.

True to her word, Sophia encourages Jarett to go with her to shop for décor for their new office design. He's hesitant to leave, but I assure him I have some calls to make and a few things to sort out before my flight. We agree to meet at Central Station at six o'clock to make our way to Maxine's for appetizers and cocktails.

Now I'm sitting in my room writing out a list of pros and cons in my notebook, putting off the phone calls. Why I insist on creating a list, I don't know, because I have no option but to stay. Unless, of course, I'm willing to resign and give up the biggest career opportunity I may ever have.

Which, I'm not.

I want this.

My career is about to move ahead in leaps and bounds. The project tasks identified in the email I received from Malcolm after our call have motivated me, kickstarted my creative juices, and amplified my love of this career choice.

Still, I continue with my list of pros and cons.

There are two cons.

One, what to do with my relationship with Jarett. Our five-night fling can't continue past tonight.

Two, I'll miss my friends.

Hardly enough cons to warrant any indecision or concern. *Right?*

My friends will still be there when I eventually

return home, we can FaceTime regularly, and I'll be giving them an excuse to come to London. Plus, I'll be able to go home for a visit inside the first twelve months. That, I'll make sure of. The Jarett situation isn't as clear because my head and heart are at war.

I push my notebook to the side and close the cover. Picking up my phone, I call my mom. Of course, she's excited for me, knowing how much my career progression means to me and how hard I've worked to get here. Given we aren't particularly close, and I don't see her as often as I should, anyway, she isn't too worried about me being on the other side of the world. Her only words of advice are to "stay true to yourself and don't let anyone take advantage."

That, I can do.

Next, I FaceTime Miah. It's midnight in Australia. *I should've made these calls earlier in the day.* She picks up on the second ring. "Hey, girl, you packed and ready to come home?" she yawns into the phone.

"Umm, nope. Not exactly, no." Her on-point greeting leaves no room for idle chit-chat, and I'm grateful. Her eyes widen, and concern etches her sleepy face.

"An incredible work opportunity has come up for me. I had a call from Malcolm this afternoon. A big-deal hotelier wants me to stay on as his hands-on consultant to help with the design and roll-out of a new hotel chain here in London."

"Eeek." Miah goes from yawn to screaming into the phone in less than five seconds. "Holy fuck, are you serious, Kassidy?" She doesn't give me time to respond before she continues with her excited rant. "That's fucking huge, congratulations! This could be the big break you've been looking for, right?"

"Exactly."

"So, you'll be what? Another week or two before you're home then?"

I let out a deep breath and rub my temples. My eyes close as I break the news. "The initial contract is for twelve months, so unless—"

"Whoa, twelve months?"

"Yeah, it's a big job, multiple hotels, and I'll be employing a team of people to help with all aspects I'm not qualified to complete myself."

She's quiet for a few moments. Her voice is strained when she eventually speaks. "I'm so proud of you, Kass. This is a major opportunity. But twelve months, I can't miss you for twelve long months. We might blow up FaceTime with how much we'll be using it now." She pushes out a light laugh, and I smile sadly.

I know how she feels. I'm a bucket of mixed emotions, especially now I've told her. "The upside is, I'll get holidays, all-expenses-paid trips home at least a few times in the year, so it won't be twelve whole months until I see you again."

"Thank fuck because that feels like a death sentence to me." Her tone is sad, and it hurts my heart.

I explain that I may come home after the initial consult to collect some of my things but wouldn't know more for at least another week. She nods, avoiding direct eye contact. Then I hear her sniffle, and she pinches the bridge of her nose, something she does when she's welling up but desperately trying not to cry.

"I love you, Mi-Mi," I tell her. "It's late for you, and I need to ring Raven and Chloe as well." Again, she nods. When she finally peers at me, there's a tear falling which I pretend not to notice.

"Love you, Kass. Talk soon, okay?"

The video call ends, and I dread making the next two calls.

The conversations with Raven and Chloe mirror the call with Miah except for one thing. A few months ago, Chloe reunited with her long-lost love, Will, and recently Raven has hooked up with a successful surgeon, Sean, and is, against all odds, now in a committed relationship. Therefore, blinded by love, their first questions centered around Jarett.

"Oh my God, you're staying in London for a guy?" Raven quips.

I laugh at the shock in her voice and ignore the surprise on her face. "Did you miss the part where

I said this is a massive career opportunity?"

She sighs. "Of course not, and I'm over-the-moon happy for you, I am. But the thought of you choosing Jarett, some five-night fling over me, sucks balls, Kassidy Rae."

I shake my head. She reminds me of my mother, who always uses my first and middle name together when I'm in trouble. "I'm not choosing anybody. It's business. I have to stay or kiss my career goodbye, which isn't an option."

She waves her hand at me. "I know, I know. I get all that. But I want it noted that although I want you to succeed, I'll miss you every second you're gone and will be counting down until we get to see you again."

Smiling, I nod as her bottom lip drops a little. "Duly noted. I'll let you know when I'll be coming home. Who knows, it may be sooner than later, but I have to wait and see what happens after the initial consultation."

Raven reminds me to stay clear of all future flings, and one-night stands are the only appropriate course of action if I were to kick ass with this contract. I didn't promise anything, but her advice on this was also noted.

Now to figure out what the hell to tell Jarett and Sophia.

Or more to the point, how much to tell them.

Chapter 19

KASSIDY

Flicking through my small closet of clothes, I can't decide what to wear to Maximum tonight. I should've been packing for an early flight out in the morning, but my world is tilted, and my mind is skewed.

After I shower and apply my makeup, I opt for the royal blue wrap dress to show off my curves. And, you guessed it, my stiletto boots.

Tomorrow I'll go shopping for more of everything once I move apartments. My love of boots is almost equal to my penchant for scarves, but unfortunately, when you're traveling light, one pair of boots is the limit.

That's another pro for my list right there. I can buy all the boots my heart desires and don't have to worry about shipping them home.

Not for a while, anyway.

This gets me thinking about what I'd want to collect or have packed up at home and shipped over to me. Most of my wardrobe will be inappropriate for London weather. My rather large lingerie collection would be nice to have, but the starting bonus will be more than enough to cater for a new lingerie collection here.

Apart from some personal mementos I'd love to have with me but wouldn't want to risk shipping in case they break or are lost in transit, I'm confident I can survive a year without it all. They'd be safer at home waiting for my return.

Dressed and ready to celebrate, I have thirty minutes before I'm due to leave to reach the subway in time. At the table, pen in hand, I begin a new list of all the things I have to organize.

It's funny, this morning, I was picturing the long flight home after saying a difficult goodbye to Jarett. I was excited about seeing my girls and starting back at the office on Wednesday.

Now, everything has changed.

Admittedly, excitement is building quickly, especially now I've made the most important calls. Tomorrow, after I spring the news on Sophia and Jarett tonight, I'll post on social media and move on with my new life in London.

A knock at the door startles me out of my dream-like state. I open the door to find Jarett, his brilliant smile and sparkling eyes staring at me, a small bag in his hand. "God, Kassidy, you look brilliant in blue. As you do in everything, but that dress is..." His words stall, but his expression says it all. "May I?" he asks, gesturing inside.

"Of course." I step aside to let him in. "I thought I was meeting you at the subway."

"Sophia will meet us there. I wanted to stop by quickly to give you a going-away gift. I didn't think you'd want to carry it with you all night." He holds the bag out, and I take it, peeking inside

"You didn't have to," I say, pulling out a gorgeous satin scarf with a bohemian style pattern with brilliant purples and teals. I'm absolutely in love. I rub the satin over my chest, not wanting to get makeup on it. "So beautiful, Jarett, thank you so much."

I move in to kiss his lips. Prolonging it a little, I squeeze his denim-clad ass cheeks, and he smiles, pulling me closer to him. "That's the best thank you, I could've hoped for."

Separating, Jarett continues, "I know how much you love scarves. Actually, I saw this particular one in a store window moments after I left here the day we met. Look at the label..." He has no idea I bought a bunch of them this morning, but a girl can never have too many. 'Kassidy Lane' is the brand on the label. It couldn't be more fitting. "I wanted to get you a thick woolen one in a deep teal that reminded me of you, but I figured you would have little use for it in Australia."

I cringe at his words. "Yeah, about that…" I take his hand and guide him to the oversized one-person sofa. Our knees touch as I sit and turn to him, his hand still in mine.

"There have been some developments today." I'm nervously tapping my toes on the floor, and Jarett steadies my leg with his hand. I have a habit of bouncing when I'm anxious.

"What sort of developments, exactly?" He narrows his eyes and cocks his head in question. I can't tell if he's simply interested or concerned about what I'm about to say.

"It turns out a client has contracted our firm…" I point at my chest with my thumb, "… aka moi, to assist with the design and roll-out of a new hotel chain in London."

I barely get the words out before Jarett is smiling like a Cheshire cat. "You're staying?" he asks, not hesitating a second.

"At this stage, yes."

He frowns and takes his hand from mine. "At this stage," he repeats the words slowly.

"I have a meeting and initial consult next weekend, so I'll know more after that. They've already sent the contract and secured me as their hands-on consultant, but it's the finer details that are a little vague. As in, I don't even know when this is due to begin. All I know is, I'll be moving to an apartment tomorrow, paid for by my company, and once I meet with the client, he'll be handing over keys to my new apartment in Shoreditch for the next twelve months."

All the words flow out in a hurry, leaving me breathless toward the end. Meanwhile, Jarett stares at me, wide-eyed and incredibly happy with this new development. I can't say I'm surprised by his reaction, but it doesn't help my situation.

"An apartment in Shoreditch? Twelve months?"

I nod slowly, a smile spreading across my lips. His excitement is contagious.

"So, you're relocating?"

"For the period of the contract, I guess. Yeah."

He glances around the room. "An apartment in Shoreditch is going to seem like a mansion compared to this room. You know you might get lost?"

I laugh out loud, grateful for the joke. "Well, I have an interim apartment for next week. I should have those details by the time I'm expected to vacate in the morning."

Jarett bounces off the sofa and tucks his hands in his pocket before turning to me, where I'm still stationed awkwardly on the edge of the cushion. "You know what this means, right?"

My heart hammers in my chest. I can't deal with any further propositions today.

With anticipation, I wait for him to speak and burst out laughing when he says, "I need to go buy that woolen teal scarf."

Pulling me to him, we stare silently at one another for a beat too long. Unspoken words hang between us in the silence. My heart hammers in my chest as he pushes my hair from my face, tucking it behind my ear. Goosebumps scatter over my exposed skin as his fingers softly trace the curve of my neck.

Slowly, Jarett guides my chin up with his fingers and caresses my lips with his in an excruciatingly beautiful kiss—sensual and full of promise. A kiss has never before held so much power over my body. This kiss is filled with all the words left unsaid and all the moments leading up to this very second. The passion is all-consuming, and I can't pull myself away.

Even if I wanted to.

When Jarett finally breaks our kiss, his erection is pressing hard against my torso, and his eyes are heavy with lust.

"We should get going, or we'll miss our ride," he whispers croakily.

His forehead rests comfortably on mine for a beat as we both struggle to gain control.

"I was starting to think you two stopped for a quickie somewhere, leaving me stranded and alone," Sophia jokes as we arrive with seconds to spare on the subway platform.

"What am I, fucking invisible?" Roman stirs from beside her, reaching out to shake Jarett's hand before taking mine and gifting it another sweet kiss.

"Wonderful to see you again, Kassidy." Roman and Jarett share a subtle exchange as we jump on the subway and settle in for our short trip.

We discuss their Wednesday and Sunday rituals at the speakeasy and the fact Roman mostly only tags along on Sundays because Monday is his one day off from Café Zest.

"I'll have you know I had planned to stop by there tomorrow morning on the way to the airport to say goodbye as I promised when we met." Roman gives me an endearing smile and informs me he'll be devastated if he misses me saying goodbye.

Sophia shoots me a hopeful glance, but Jarett begins to rile Roman up about his on-again-off-again attraction to Maxine before she can ask what's on her mind. I feign shock at this information about Roman and Maxine as if it weren't easy to spot the first time I saw them together. Roman ignores us as we laugh and joke about his obsession.

"Honestly, though..." I add seriously, "... you two seem perfect together."

Sophia and Jarett look at me like I've emerged from a sewer.

"What?"

Roman lets out a hearty laugh that catches the attention of nearby passengers on the tube.

I'm oblivious to their inside joke until Sophia speaks up, "Maxine and Roman had a thing quite some years ago. You know Maxine has been part of our family since we were kids since our parents and hers were remarkably close. Roman used to always say he'd marry Maxine, and he even proposed to her in third grade." Sophia laughs as she squeezes Roman's leg in jest.

"I believe she nut-sacked him for that proposal and each one after that," Jarett adds. Roman scowls, and the three of us erupt in another fit of laughter.

"There was more than one proposal?" His eyes soften when they reach mine, and slowly his scowl turns into a smile, followed by a lighthearted chuckle.

"Bastards."

Sophia nudges me as Roman and Jarett continue their brother banter. "You said you had planned to stop at Zest tomorrow..." she burrows closer into my side and whispers, her eyes darting between her brothers. "Does that mean you're *not* leaving tomorrow?"

Happiness bubbles from within until I can no longer conceal my smile. As happy as a kid in a candy store, I clasp her hands with mine and whisper, "Nope, I'll be here for your birthday."

Cue the squeals.

Jarett and Roman spin in our direction, alarmed by the noisy commotion. "Kassidy is staying for my birthday party! This is the best birthday present ever, isn't it?"

Sophia's energy is outrageously contagious. I foresee spending a lot of time with her over the coming year.

Jarett laughs quietly and squeezes my knee. "Yes, it's the best news I've ever heard."

"You told him before me?" Sophia pretends to be hurt, and both brothers shake their heads at her.

"How did you manage that mere hours before you were due to fly out?"

Coyly, I shrug in Roman's direction. "Some things just fall into place when you want them to, I guess."

Sophia fills them in on how she *begged* me to reconsider leaving. She has no idea everything was already set in motion before her invitation, but I don't want to take away her sense of importance.

Jarett, however, insists on giving all the details.

"But did she tell you the best part, sis?"

Her eyes fly open. Sitting forward in her seat, her eyes flash between all of us. "There's more?"

Subtle movements, I was learning, aren't Sophia's strong suit. She claps her hands together loudly and bounces in her seat like an oversized child. "OMG, are you moving here?"

I can't help but giggle. What a great guest-imator she is. "For twelve months, yes, I'll be living and working here."

She throws herself at me, her arms wrapping tight around my shoulders. "How in the fuck did you pull that one off so swiftly? Girl, do you have your boss eating out of your hand or what?"

I fill them in on the details, the basics of what I know, anyway.

"Depending on where you'll be stationed for work, that will mean we're all working in Central London and living in Shoreditch."

Right now, I'm not quite as excited as the rest of them. Ending things with Jarett could potentially ruin more than just our friendship. I've grown fond of Sophia over the past few days, and Jarett, well, the words which come to mind for him terrify me, if I'm honest. And Roman, who I've only seen on two occasions, I can tell he's fun, honest, and good company.

My own little UK family.

Who am I to ruin a good thing because I want to

progress with my career? Ugh.

On the upside, I don't have to make any decisions tonight. Until I do, I'm going to give myself the go-ahead to live it up.

No questions asked.

No, what-ifs or maybes.

"I believe we have something well worth toasting tonight, folks," Jarett announces, holding his glass high in the center of the table. Maxine has Sundays off from the bar, so she's joined the group.

Roman and Maxine share a strange vibe, a kind of comfortable awkwardness if you can call it that. Sitting directly opposite each other, they badly attempt to avoid eye contact unless they think nobody is watching.

"To Kassidy, welcome to London and congratulations on the new contract. I know you'll do an outstanding job, and I'm happier than a pig in shit that you'll be gracing us all with your presence for the next year."

We toast, and I thank everyone for their kindness before I relax and enjoy my mad-as-fuck cocktail which has steam flowing from the edges of the glass. I love this speakeasy and feel right at home here.

"Just don't ruin it for us, bro," Sophia jokes, and I almost spit up my drink.

Jarett hands me a napkin without meeting my eyes. "I don't plan on ruining a thing. Friendships will not be handled harshly."

As I look at him, I see the meaning in his words. He doesn't want me to feel compelled or for this fling to feel like it's automatically more than it is because I'm staying.

I lean in and kiss him. "Thank you," I whisper.

"I've got you, sweetheart. Anyway, you'll let me, but I'll be devastated if a friendship as good as this is ever off the cards for us."

I bring his lips to mine again, my hands clasped around his face. "As would I," I confide in him between kisses.

"Enough already, you have plenty of time for that now. Tonight, let's drink." Sophia's outburst is well received, and drink is exactly what we do.

Until the early hours of Monday morning.

Chapter 20

JARETT

"Drinking on a school night is a bad idea, little bro," Sophia slurs as we finally leave the speakeasy. The narrow and windy stairs with two very tipsy women on my arm is a tricky feat—two steps up, three steps back.

But we make it.

Eventually.

"I'm making a judgment call and saying you're both coming home with me," I tell them as we hit the sidewalk. A man and woman walking toward us glance between Sophia and Kassidy and grace me with a dirty look.

I could've jumped on that and explained my life away, but what would be the point of that? Instead, there will be two strangers walking the streets and telling their mates tomorrow that a drunk guy was taking advantage of two beautiful women when they could barely walk.

There could be worse things to be said about me, but luckily these two beauties know and trust me.

Once we arrive at my apartment because mine is a few blocks closer than Sophia's, and Roman left a few hours ago, Kassidy helps me as much as she can while swaying all over the place to get Sophia into bed. When she's securely tucked away in the guest room, Kassidy starts to undress in the lounge room.

Amused, I observe her from the sofa as she hops around on one foot, trying to free the other from her boot. She's talking gibberish about her flight home, which she's no longer on. It's comical as hell, but I worry she might fall and break her ankle, or worse, fall headfirst into the plate glass window.

"Come here, love. Let me help you." She holds her arms out wide as I approach and falls into my chest. Wrapping my arms around her waist, her delicate laugh filters through the semi-darkness in a perfect melody.

I don't want to let her go.

Tonight is supposed to be our fifth and final night together. I want nothing more for her to stay, to see where this thing goes between us, but I also don't want her to feel obligated. One thing is for certain, though. I meant what I told her earlier in the evening. I never want our friendship to be lost. She has very quickly become one of my most favorite people in my life.

There's a sense of knowing and general comfort with Kassidy that I've never experienced with another person, male or female. And I don't want to lose it.

And I'm not some pompous dick who assumes our relationship will continue as it started just because she's staying.

I respect she has goals and wants to pursue her career and build a name for herself. And I'll do whatever I can to support her from any place in her life. There are conversations we need to have when she's sober but not tonight.

"Can we go to bed now?" she whispers into my neck.

"Of course, beautiful."

I steady her on her feet as best I can with her dress hanging open from one side, one boot off, the other undone and partially removed. Picking her up, I cradle her to my chest and carry her to the bedroom.

Maybe one day it will be *our* bedroom.

Laying Kassidy on the bed, I remove the second boot and rub her feet. She's out cold, but it doesn't stop me from admiring her. Finding a spare tee in the closet, I awkwardly remove the dress without tearing it. How women get in and out of these fucking things is beyond me.

"It's okay, love," I whisper as she squirms,

making it difficult for me to take her arms out of the sleeves. "I'm taking your dress off, so you sleep comfortably." Honestly, I doubt it matters what she's wearing. At this point, I suspect she'll sleep just as soundly on the hardwood floor. Once I have the shirt partially on, I unfasten the front clip on her bra and leave her panties on.

I don't want Kassidy to wake in the morning thinking I took advantage of her while she was too wasted to know what was happening.

I'm a lot of things, but an asshole who disrespects women will never be one of them. Turning the lights off once she's situated under the covers, I crawl into bed and wrap her in my arms. She murmurs contentedly when I pull her closer, then proceeds to snore.

I've never known a woman to snore, though my wife is the only other woman I have ever spent an entire night in bed with. Even in college, I was never in a serious enough relationship to justify a sleepover.

Kassidy's steady rumbles are quite relaxing once she gets into a rhythm. I'm not sure how long I lay there listening to her before I finally drift off to sleep, but like the other nights we have been together, I have the best sleep.

KASSIDY

Gremlins in my head are having a dance-off and kicking the shit out of my brain. My skull aches, a full three-sixty degrees of hurt. I groan in agony as I roll to my side. That's when I notice a hand wrapped around me. A warm body embraces mine, providing protection but taking away none of the pain.

"Mmm."

A sweet peck on the back of my neck has my eyes fluttering open.

"Ugh," I moan.

The light is too much. I squeeze my eyes closed and vow to try again later.

I feel his body shuddering behind me, then I hear a distinct chuckle. The motherfucker is laughing at me.

"You feel a little under the weather, my love?" he taunts.

"Na," I lie with all the energy I have left.

I must have dozed off again because the next thing I know, he's standing over the bed with a large mug of caffeine, a cold bottle of water, and some pills. *Give me those pills.*

"Here you go, beautiful. Some Advil and caffeine will have you back up and running in no time." Even though he smirks at me, I can sense he wants to say so much more.

Sitting up, I throw my legs from under the covers to the floor at the side of the bed. Clutching my head between both hands, I try to stop it from rolling down the hall. My mouth tastes like I fell asleep feasting on mothballs and candy. I am terrified to wrap my lips around the bottle of water in case I infect it.

Charming as fuck.

I twist my face as I skull the remains of the bottle after taking my pills. I must admit the headache is mild in comparison to earlier. With poorly focused vision, I glance around. *What the hell is the time?*

"Your phone is in the kitchen charging, and it's half-past eight," Jarett answers, reading my mind.

"Thank you," I respond, taking the coffee from his hands.

"Where's Sophia?" I hope she makes it to the office in time.

Jarett smiles, oblivious to the fact I'm feeling awful, and we all stayed and got so fucked up last night. "She was gone when I got up. Don't worry about her, she sets her own schedule at the office."

Jarett disappears to the bathroom, and the water starts running. "I think you deserve a bubble bath to relax in, while your coffee kicks in. How's that sound?"

"Fucking delightful."

I stand slowly and look down at the shirt I'm wearing. *Wasted* is written across the front in bold letters, and I laugh until my brain vibrates from the movement. "I thought it was fitting... considering."

I cover my eyes. "Ugh, I'm sorry. Did you dress me?"

"Yes. I undressed you, too, but I remained quite the gentleman, I promise."

"I wouldn't doubt it for a second."

Chapter 21

KASSIDY

Once again, I wake up in Shoreditch, change into last night's clothes, and have to catch the subway home like a dirty tramp. And I don't give an ounce of fucks. In another week, I'll be able to go back to my apartment close to the speakeasy. I'm more excited about the move today than I was yesterday, even with a hangover from hell.

"Thank you for the spare toothbrush. I don't think I could survive another second without one," I joke. "I really should get back to my room and pack my things." Pulling up my emails on my phone, I add, "I should probably find out where I'm moving to, I guess."

Jarett grabs me from behind and spins me around to face him, pushing me against the island in the kitchen. "I have a meeting at the gallery at ten, but I can head over afterward to help with your stuff if you want," he says this while nuzzling my neck, his woody aftershave invigorating my senses.

"Yes, I whisper." Wait. I shake my head to clear out the static. "No!" I laugh, "I don't need any help. I have the same luggage I arrived with, plus an extra shopping bag or two. I can get a town car to my next destination and text you the address, so you know where to find me." I reach up on my tiptoes and kiss him.

"Mm..." he moans into my lips, both of us smiling and not wanting to let go.

"Do you want me to be able to find you, Kassidy?" His voice is deeper than usual, and it arouses me.

I close my eyes and pull him into a hug, scared to look at him the way I'm feeling at the moment. "Yes, Jarett, I think I do."

"Okaaay," he says, stringing out the letters. "You let me know if you start to *think* differently at any time. Agreed?"

Chuckling, I agree. "You promised whatever happens, we'll remain friends, right?"

"Always," he whispers, planting another kiss on my lips before letting me go.

It was only then I notice the new additions to the apartment.

"Jarett," I say as he's almost out of the kitchen. He spins around. "You've started to move into the apartment finally?"

"Yes. I thought it was time." He smiles slightly and rubs the back of his neck before he disappears down the hall.

On our way to the city, Jarett explains the movers came on Friday to pack up his home in Soho and prepare his wife's belongings to be shipped to her parents in Italy. He hired a decorator to decorate the apartment with his choice of colors and design to make it feel like a home much different than he shared with Helena. All his items are now in his new apartment.

"I'm free of that part of my life now. I'll never forget or regret a moment of it, but it's in the past, and I'm ready to move on." This pleases me so much. Jarett deserves a life of love and joy after enduring so much pain and sorrow. I squeeze his hand resting in mine and has been for the duration of the trip so far.

"I'm so happy for you, Jarett. You deserve to move forward and live your life." I rest my head on his shoulder, and we sit in silence the rest of the way.

As we walk off the subway platform, people rush past us eager to get to work or wherever they are headed, and Jarett pulls me to the side.

"I couldn't have done this without you, Kassidy. I hope you understand what it means to me." I know what he's referring to, but it's not my doing. This is all on him. "Meeting you, a woman I can be myself around without limitation or judgment, it's restored my faith in women and helped me to move forward."

"You're welcome, Jarett, but you're stronger than you believe. You should give yourself more credit."

My new apartment is first-class compared to the tiny shoebox at the Country Inn. It comes fully self-contained with bright artwork on the walls, abstract vases, and statues adorning the floors and shelves. With colorful throw rugs and cushions on the sofa, it looks like a unicorn threw up—in the best way.

I see myself at home here, but there's no point in getting attached when I'll have to do this all over again in a week.

Thanks to Malcolm and his clever thinking, he secured me this place in Shoreditch, knowing it's where I'll end up. For all I know, the apartment may be in this building.

After unpacking my clothes, I tap out a quick text to Sophia. One, to see how she pulled through, and two, tell her where my interim home is located. I'm dying to know how far I am from her. I'm a few blocks from Jarett's apartment, and so is she, but I'm not sure in which direction.

The dots bounce across the screen as Sophia drafts a response.

> **Sophia**: *Feel like roadkill – is that what you Aussies would say?*

The bitch, she makes me laugh.

> **Kassidy**: *Close enough lol*

Another message follows quickly after.

> **Sophia**: *You're on the same block as me! Opposite ends!*

I fist pump the air and let out a squeal.

> **Sophia**: *What apartment? I'll stop by on the way home for wine and scrummy nosh. Can we eat in?*

Gah, the British lingo. Both Jarett and Sophia are over the top with it. They believe I should be localized and learn the lingo. So yeah, insert delicious food. Eating in sounds brilliant. I have a whole years' worth of nights to indulge in the nightlife, and I'm in no rush to get out. An early night in is exactly what I need.

> **Kassidy**: *Yes, let's do it.*

One problem. I have zero food and no local

knowledge of grocers.

Kassidy: *Uber Eats, okay?*

A thumbs-up response comes through as I'm messaging Jarett. I have plenty of time to go to the store, but truthfully, I can't be fucked. Still basking in the effects of the bubble bath Jarett ran for me this morning, I'm considering another in my new tub.

Okay, in the spa bath. Not an ordinary tub.

I'm not sure whether to invite Jarett for dinner or whether Sophia wants a girls' night. But when he messages back, he mentions Uber Eats, so crisis diverted. Sophia must have told him. Not for the first time, it crosses my mind that Sophia is more invested in the outcome of our relationship than either of us are.

Only time will tell, and there's no point fretting the small stuff. For now, I'll embrace my new life to the fullest.

Sophia shows up before Jarett with a basket full of

snacks. All of London's best, she assures me. "Woman, you didn't have to do that. I thought you felt like roadkill." I laugh.

"I didn't go out of my way, I assure you. Our clients bring in so many of these things a week, I have half an office full of the shit."

She places the basket on the bench and kisses me hello. "Give me the tour," she cheers. "I can't believe we're on the same block. Is this the same block of apartments you'll be in for the length of your stay?"

"Honestly, I have no idea. I've not had any contact with the hotelier yet. I'm waiting on an email with instructions about where to meet this weekend, but more exciting than that, is your birthday."

"Yes, I can't wait." She fills me in on all the details. Fancy dress, Gatsby style in a private event at the speakeasy.

"Two hundred people?"

I imagine us dancing like tinned sardines at Maxine's, but she assures me their biggest nights have hosted two hundred and fifty plus.

"Okay, you're on. But there's one problem."

"I have Friday off to prepare," she cuts me off. "We'll shop for your outfit and enjoy an afternoon at the spa with some of my girlfriends after that."

Sophia is all over this. She's an avid planner, and I love that about her.

"It will be a great opportunity to meet some of

my circle of friends before the night."

Jarett texts to say he's ten minutes away if we need anything. It's only half-past five, so we decide to crack a bottle of wine that was in the fridge when I arrived. When Jarett gets here, we'll decide on the dinner menu.

"Full disclosure," Sophia adds, plopping down on the sofa beside me. "Bella is a good friend of mine, and she's been hot for Jarett since high school. She probably won't appreciate your relationship with him very much."

"Should I stay clear? Is she contagious?"

"She's a catty attention-seeker, but I've known her forever. We just nod, agree, and ignore. But if she's less inviting than the others, that's why."

"Thanks for the heads-up. I don't see why a fling with Jarett would cause any issues, though," I respond, taking a sip of the wine, savoring it in my mouth.

"You're still calling it a fling, then?" Smiling, she observes me over the rim of her glass.

"We both agreed a five-night fling would be the most it would ever be," I answer pointedly, not sure now is the right time to enter this discussion.

"Yet, this will be night six, and he's joining us for dinner." She bats her eyelids innocently at me.

I fake a cough. "And I believe that was your doing."

"Maybe, but can you honestly say you wouldn't

have seen him tonight? Shown off the new apartment, broken it in, perhaps?"

"I plead the fifth."

Saved by the bell.

Literally.

Jarett swoops in with a large arrangement of flowers, greeting me with a peck on the cheek on his way past. "Honey, I'm home," he yells.

I spin on my heels to find Sophia giving me the eye from the living room, snickering at Jarett's greeting. Rolling my eyes, I follow Jarett to the kitchen, where he places the box of flowers.

"These are beautiful," I tell him, rolling my fingers over the petals. "I'll grab a vase when I go out tomorrow."

"No need, that's why I got the self-watering ones in the box, so you don't have to worry about them."

This man, he thinks of everything.

"So, ladies, I looked after you both last night and today, and I've had one hell of a day in the art world. What's for dinner? I'm buying."

"You are not," I scold him. "This is my home, and dinner is on me. Thank you very much."

"Exactly. My buying dinner is your housewarming gift. No arguing, it's already decided."

There's no point discussing this further, he'll always win. I can't let him continue this, though. Five nights is one thing but treating me everywhere we go for the rest of the year could be a libido killer.

"Well, if you're paying, I'm choosing. You both like Indian?"

Sophia laughs. "You can't ask questions now, you said it's your decision." She tsks me playfully, and Jarett agrees with his earth-altering grin.

I ignore them both. "Indian it is. What's the best place around here for a spicy Rogan josh?" I typically enjoy a night in with Indian curries at least once every ten days back home, and I'm not stopping now. Indian is my comfort food, and although I had a quiet and non-eventful day, I'm feeling exhausted all the same. I want to lounge on my new sofa, curl up under the afghan put some boring television series on, and fall asleep.

"Kassidy, Naan bread?" Jarett asks with the phone in his hand.

"Garlic cheese, please."

I refill our wine glasses and pour one for Jarett too. He pinches my ass on my way past him to hand Sophia hers. I draw back the blinds in the room to look out at the night view. It isn't as nice as looking out over the London Eye, but there was a lot to see in Shoreditch. The murals and artwork on the shop fronts brighten the street, and people mill below us on the sidewalks.

"Kassidy, love." I turn at the sound of Jarett's voice. "Dinner will be here in thirty minutes. Care to show me around?"

"Absolutely." I lead him to the back of the apartment to show him the master bedroom first.

"Did I interrupt something between you and Sophia when I arrived?" he whispers in my ear. A look of concern clouds his eyes, and I assure him he didn't. There wasn't much to show him in terms of rooms. I imagine he knew this already but was wanting to get me away from his sister to pry.

"Wow, you've got a spa bath?"

"It's lovely, too," I confirm.

"You had two soaks in the tub in one day?" He laughs.

"What can I say, I'm a spoiled bitch on an extended holiday."

Besides the small guest room, there's only the kitchen, living space, and the foyer which is an overly large area filled with attractive but useless dust-collecting floor ornaments.

"It's good to see you haven't lost your way in all this extra square footage," he jokes as we finish the mini-tour. I mock him and reach for him without thinking.

My fingertips graze his arm before I quickly retract my reach. It didn't go unnoticed by Jarett. He flinches, and a slight burrow of his brow appears before Sophia averts the attention from me to her.

I'm officially a fan of Masala on Fifth. My Rogan Josh is filthy hot and has me sweating up a storm. Thankfully, Jarett thought to order another bottle of wine to enjoy with our food.

Soon after we finish up, Sophia prepares to leave, looking to crash in bed early after last night's shenanigans. Feigning a slight headache, I mention an early night too.

Sophia flings a questioning glance in Jarett's direction before she kisses us both goodbye and sees herself out. "Friday, we're shopping, don't forget!"

I wave goodnight, yelling, "I can't wait."

There's an uncomfortable silence between Jarett and me once Sophia leaves, and I hate it. It's as if we're driving along the edge of a cliff, and a rockslide has blocked our path. Neither of us knows whether to take the plunge into the dark ocean waters or turn back around.

"You look exhausted," Jarett says, taking my hand and rubbing my knuckles in small circles.

"Is that code for *you look like shit, Kassidy*?"

Shaking his head side to side, he lifts my hand to his mouth, planting a lingering kiss. "There's no such thing where you're concerned, Miss Moore."

A warmth spreads through my body at his use of my surname in that context. Would it be bad to take him to bed and cuddle up with him for the night? I'm too tired for anything more than a cuddle which makes him staying a very bad idea.

Avoiding any further emotional connection is for the best. To spend nights together *sleeping* but not *fucking* would be harder than fucking his brains out and sending him home.

"I should go and let you enjoy your new digs," Jarett adds before I can say anything further. My heart pings with disappointment, but I know it's for the best. For both of us.

For a few moments, we stare at each other, neither wanting to be the one to turn away.

"Thank you for the flowers and dinner." I go to kiss his cheek, but he catches me off guard, and our lips meet in a fiery explosion. Time stands still as we pour everything we are, all that we feel, and all the words left unsaid into our kiss. We moan, chasing the next wave of lust with every swirl of our tongues. We lap at each other like immature teenagers making out under the bleachers at the high school dance. Our breaths quicken, and a gasp escapes my lips as Jarett's hands explore beneath my clothes.

I'm about to march him to my room and throw him on my bed when he pulls back, starry-eyed like a bucket of ice water landed on his head. "I'm so sorry, Kassidy, I didn't mean..."

"Me either, my fault," I say, not entirely sure what we're apologizing for.

Jarett drags his hand through his thick hair, his eyes hooded. "I should go."

"Sure, okay," I answer, my game face on.

I follow him to the door, where he kisses my lips

as a best friend would.

    As he retreats down the corridor and out of view, I'm left wondering what the fuck happened.

Chapter 22

KASSIDY

Too exhausted to make sense of anything, I take a bottle of water from the fridge, flick off the lights, and curl into my freshly made bed, where I am sure to fall asleep in minutes.

Only the minutes turn into hours, and I'm more awake now than I had been before we ordered dinner. I could blame the strange bed, but I travel too much without complaint for that to be a thing.

I miss him. Picking up my phone, my finger hovers over his name. Resisting, I place the phone face down on the side table until I can no longer stand the deafening silence.

"Hey, Siri," I speak from the darkness, waking my phone. "Play music on Spotify."

Immediately, my last playlist begins to play, the one I was listening to when trying to sleep on the flight from Prague to London six days ago. I reduce the volume and change sides, kicking off the blanket and twisting one foot out from under the sheet. Almost comfortable enough to relax, I puff up the pillows beneath my head and put another between my thighs like a cuddle buddy. I wind my arm around another and crush it to me.

My eyelids are heavy, and my thoughts a blur as sleep pulls me closer.

Until my phone beeps and vibrates loudly on the table, launching me six inches off the bed in fright.

Jarett: *I hate that I'm missing you in my bed.*

Ahhh, and therein lies the problem for both of us.

Six nights in London. Four spent with Jarett. How the hell can four nights in a man's arms make one night without him sleepless, restless, and lonely?

At what point in less than a week could we possibly have reached a place where we hate to sleep without the other?

The following day, I focus on creating a new life for myself. I explore new areas of the neighborhood, find a new favorite place to get an early morning coffee fix, and check out a few of the nearby gyms. Until I decide on a gym to call home, I'll stick with morning runs on the streets of

Shoreditch, which are full of life and artistic inspiration.

I find a fresh food market on my run where I visit and acquire a good haul of food to cook at home. No longer on vacation means regular home-cooked meals, exercise regime, hobbies, and friends.

I've been speaking with Miah, Raven, and Chloe daily and waiting patiently for the email to arrive from Mr. Gabe Lugreno, so I know what to expect when we meet. In the meantime, I extensively research all his projects to date, including business acquisitions, partnerships, and every possible detail which is publicly available and recorded online.

Tuesday evening, I visit some of his hotels and competitors to acquaint myself with their design and atmosphere. Focusing on my purpose and the reason I'm still in London helps to keep my mind free of Jarett. It doesn't always work, but it helps.

Kinda.

Okay, not really.

Yep, not at all.

I often wonder what he's doing and how he's spending his nights. He checks in with me at least once I day, but I always end up saying I'm busy tying up loose ends for clients back home. It's not a lie, but I could fit in a visit with him any time.

After the way he left on Monday night, I figured some space between us would be best. Of course, we'll be seeing each other on Saturday at Sophia's birthday party. Secretly, I'm more excited to see Jarett than anything else.

Tomorrow is Friday, the day Sophia is helping to find an outfit for her special evening and introducing me to her click of gal pals. It will be great to meet some new people because I'm desperately missing my tribe. Trying not to think too much about what I miss the most, I reroute my thoughts to all the fun and adventures that lay ahead.

But all I see is Jarett.

I hadn't heard from Sophia since the first night in my new apartment, so I tap out a quick text to confirm where I should meet her on Friday.

Her response was short and sweet.

Sophia: *At yours at 10 a.m.*

Not long after, I'm sitting in a café in the burrows reading a book. An actual paperback I picked up from an indie bookstore on my way. Reading fiction of any kind is something I haven't done in so long, I wasn't sure it would hold my attention.

I'm fully invested until I receive a text message.

Jarett: *You're looking as beautiful as ever. What are you reading?*

Quickly, I spin around in my chair, looking every which way for the man I dream about night and day but haven't seen for two and a half days. But who's counting, right?

Seconds later, he walks into the café with a dazzling smile and a buoyant attitude. Coming to stand at my booth, he gestures to the seat opposite me. "May I?"

"Of course." When he sits, I have to tie my tongue to refrain from word vomiting on him. Ever since I arrived in London, he's been there for me to share everything with, and these past sixty-something hours have been hectic and every new experience I imagine telling Jarett when I get home in the evenings.

"I've missed you." I smile at him, my entire body relaxing with his presence.

"Really? Because I was starting to think you were flipping me off. I was beginning to get a complex."

"Is that why you took up stalking lonely single women reading books in cafés?"

A devilish smile spreads across his face, his stubble darker and thicker than I'd seen before. He's a little dark under the eyes too.

"One of the reasons," he answers cheekily.

He looks around the café. The décor is bold bohemian which suits me to a tee, though quite different from his usual surroundings. "This is the first café I stopped at when I moved over this way," he tells me. "How strange that I'd find you here. Kind of reminds me how much we have in common."

His bottom lip twitches as he tries to hold back a grin. "You like the bold color, cluttered ornaments, and mismatched patterns too?"

I pick him more for the serious, sleek, and clean-cut style.

"You forget I'm an artist these past few days?"

I laugh. "Never. Have you been doing any artistic things?"

"During my lonely evenings, I set up a drawing room in the third guest room of the apartment. Bought some new tools of the trade and colors I feel accentuate my muse."

His muse.

"Excellent, and is your muse happy with the work you've created thus far?" The words taste bitter on my tongue, and the jealousy that laces each one doesn't go unnoticed.

Silently he keeps me waiting, an unreadable look on his face. "Green looks good on you, Kassidy."

Ugh. Wiseass.

I scoff, my face growing redder by the second. "Whatever gets you off," I tease.

He rolls his eyes and stands. "I stopped by my muse's place on the way here actually, but there was no answer. Imagine my surprise when I found her in my favorite coffee joint reading romance."

With that said, he strides confidently to the counter to place an order. My eyes follow him, my mind spinning.

I'm his muse.

Wait? How did he know I'm reading romance?

I look at the cover, a man and woman in a tender embrace. Hmm, wherever he was when he messaged, he must have been close enough to see it.

Glancing over at him, he points in my direction, and the waitress scribbles down his order, throwing me a polite smile.

"What did you say to her?" I demand as he joins me again.

"I ordered us both a coffee. By the sounds of it, you've been a little light on the caffeine lately."

My eyebrows arch in surprise at his observation. "Plus, I told her whenever you come in to make sure they add an extra shot of espresso to your order."

I chuckle. "You're obnoxious sometimes. And how did you know I was reading a romance book?"

Jarett shrugs. "Good guess."

Our coffee orders arrive, and we continue chatting with a healthy dose of banter.

"Why did you stop by my place, anyway?" I question, remembering what he said earlier.

"It's get-together night at the speakeasy, and I wanted to make sure you remembered."

Nope, I didn't remember. That means I've been here for a full week and, I glance at my phone, a half day. Wow, so much has changed in my life in such a short time.

"It would've completely escaped me, so thank you for that. Are you sure you want me to tag along?"

"I wouldn't call it tagging along, Kassidy. Unless you're opposed to going, I expect you to be joining us. You're part of our world now, too, and as you're a local to boot, it should be front and center on your calendar commitments."

"Is that so?"

This guy. He drives every part of me completely bonkers with lust. He's sweet, sensitive, bossy, and funny.

What more could an Aussie girl want?

Chapter 23

KASSIDY

To ascertain my independence, I opt to meet the others at Maximum instead of going with them. I hate relying on other people, especially men, for company, a good time, or an invitation.

It's quiet when I arrive, which is what I was hoping for. Maxine has intrigued me both times I've met her, and while I don't want to pry or get up in her business, I want to get to know her outside of the usual group.

"Kassidy, love. Great to see you sober," she jokes as I sit opposite her at the bar.

I groan, covering my face. "Don't remind me."

She frowns. "You're meeting Sophia and the crew, yeah?"

"Yeah, had some spare time on my hands, so I thought I'd pop in a bit earlier."

Max calls out to Danni, a younger version of herself. "Danni, meet Kassidy."

"Hi, Kassidy," she offers sweetly. "I recall you from the other night with Sophia and Jarett."

One drunken night and nobody is willing to let it go?

Note to self—*drink more water, drink fewer cocktails.*

"Nice to meet you," I offer, extending my hand.

"Danni has been with us the past few years, but she's moving up north next week, leaving me understaffed and overextended," Max offers, her hand on her hip.

It's obvious Max thinks the world of Danni and vice versa.

"Oh, what a shame."

"Anyway, what can I get you tonight?"

Think mild, Kassidy.

"A classic marg for starters, please."

She juggles the glassware and starts mixing.

The band starts up behind us, a bluesy tune echoing from their instruments.

"This is a great place, Max."

"Thanks. It's my baby. My life." She studies me intently as I follow her fluid movements of shaking the margarita and straining it into a large cocktail glass. "Can you pour a drink, Kassidy?"

The question takes me by surprise. "Yeah, I used to work the bars back home when I was putting myself through college." I scope out the bar. "Never in a lavish place like this, though... more the local pub scene with a few basic cocktails and spirits. You know."

"I often find the types who make the best cocktails are those who have an artistic flair and, most of all, love to drink them. I see you as fitting both those categories." Smiling, she hands me the margarita.

I reach into my shoulder bag for my phone to fix up the bill, but she waves it away. "The first one is on me. It's a friend-with-benefits bonus system," she adds with a laugh.

She skips along the bar to serve the next person in line when Danni stops by. With her arms on the bar, she leans closer. Quietly, she speaks with her hands cupped at each side of her mouth. "I think Max has her eye on you for my replacement." She winks at me and disappears before I can comprehend what she said.

Maxine swings by when the rest of the customers have been served, and she starts on my next drink. Another of the same. "So, I'm running a cocktail training early tomorrow morning for all my staff. You interested in joining us?"

"You need a guinea pig for taste testing?"

Maxine bubbles over with laughter. "Nah, I was thinking more along the lines of offering you a job at the bar to coincide with your day job."

"Wow, um, I'm honored. I'd certainly appreciate the opportunity, but…" I take the drink and tap into my phone to activate payment. Again, she waves it off.

"May I ask, why me?"

"Simple." She waves her index finger up and down at me, "Physically, you appeal to my customers. You're gorgeous and Australian. Men will fall in love with your accent, want to spend more time at the bar, and therefore buy more drinks and… you're funny. Full of spunk, I like to call it. Plus, you don't look like you'd take no shit from anyone."

That just about sums me up. Though I don't agree with her beauty classification, I'll take it. The job will be perfect for me, and while I have nothing else to fill my time, the additional income is hard to pass up. While I'm living abroad, I want to make the most of traveling throughout Europe. It's much more cost-effective to do it from here than it ever would be from home.

"Sold. What time should I be here tomorrow?"

"Training starts at seven, and you can do the eleven to five shift following that as your trial. If we're both happy, you're on the payroll. Cool?"

"I'm in!" I reach across the bar to shake her hand.

"You've made my day, Kassidy. I look forward to working with you."

Who needs a margarita to create a little extra

buzz in your life?

Maxine waves over my shoulder at Sophia, Jarett, and Roman. "This girl got a start on you guys. I like her."

"Working with you. Wait, what did we miss exactly?" Jarett questions with concern etched in his brow.

Greetings flow, kisses and hugs are plentiful, and even Jarett gives me a peck on the lips, causing my body to quiver with need.

"Now tell me, what did Max mean about working with you?"

All eyes turn to me. "I may have agreed to a trial run in the bar tomorrow. If all goes well, you'll be looking at the newest member of Maximum," I boast all la-di-da.

Sophia is naturally excited for me, Roman congratulates me, and Jarett, nah, he's not having it.

As he opens his mouth to give his opinion, Max pipes in while she's making drinks for the group, "Jarett Christopher Evans, she is a grown-ass woman who does not need nor desire a man's approval." She glances at me for confirmation. "Isn't that right, Kassidy?"

"Couldn't have said it better myself," I answer, staring directly at Jarett, daring him to open his mouth.

He holds my stare, his mouth itching to speak, but he relents. That is until we take our drinks to the usual booth. "You can't be serious? Working in a bar when you just took on a major new contract?"

I shrug nonchalantly. "It's extra cash, I enjoy bar work, and this place is gorgeous. Besides, it's a lot less rowdy than previous places I've worked."

Jarett continues to look at me as if I've lost my mind.

"Jarett, I know what I'm doing. Relax."

"Do you?"

One thing guaranteed to get my back up is questioning the validity of my own fucking decisions. "Did you just question my ability to make decisions for myself?" I put my drink on the table and scoot across the booth to allow him in. Although right now, I don't wish to be that close to him.

"What about the hotelier contract?"

"Many people have two jobs, Jarett. If I didn't travel so much for work back home, I'd still be working nights at the bar. Because. I. Enjoy. It. And I want to." I emphasize the words, hoping he'll take the hint and end this conversation, but he continues.

"For fuck's sake, Jarett. You're not her keeper. Kassidy is more than capable of managing her own life." I was surprised to hear Sophia jump in on the conversation, though I knew she was following our exchange from the opposite side of the booth.

Although I'm happy she's not siding with her

brother on his outrageous outburst, I also don't need her to come to my rescue. I attempt to direct my attention to the others and forget about tomorrow and Jarett's opinions.

As the group mingles and laughter ensues, I notice Jarett is less chatty than usual and spends most of his time staring at his glass. I've never seen this side of him, and I don't care for it either. Soon, he makes his way to the bar and sits estranged from us for the rest of the evening.

Waving my goodbyes to everyone and kissing Sophia, I make an early escape. "Ignore Jarett, he cares for you," she promises me. "His feelings are displaced right now, but he'll come to see that."

I thank her. I'm looking forward to my early morning run, and I've had enough for one night.

I intend to stop by the bar and say goodnight to Jarett too, but the closer I get, the clearer it becomes. Maxine is nodding and half-listening to him ramble on about men throwing themselves at female bartenders as she pours drinks and serves her patrons. I stop short of interrupting his rant and wave to her as I head back toward the stairs.

My phone rings a few times after I crawl into bed, so I silence it and turn on some music. No good will come from answering a drunken call from Jarett tonight. We do need to talk about his reaction and maybe set some ground rules for the changes in our relationship.

Chapter 24

KASSIDY

The mornings are icy cold, and the wind burns my skin as I run through the streets, but still, sweat drips from my hair beneath my beanie. Taking the elevator up to my fourth-floor apartment, I remove my AirPods, and as I walk out into the foyer on my floor, I see Jarett resting on the floor beside my door.

His head snaps up as the elevator doors ping. Scrambling to get off the floor and look half decent, I deliver a blow with a smile. "Good morning, male chauvinist of the year. What can I do you for?" Teasing him is the best way I know to break the ice and let him know I'm upset with him. His behavior, yes, but I know whatever he's feeling or thinking, his heart is in the right place.

His head falls forward, and he tucks his hands

into the pockets of his jeans. I unlock the door and am partway inside when he finally speaks. "Kassidy?"

"Yes, Jarett?" I answer quietly.

"I owe you a very large apology for last night."

The look on his face could melt the Antarctic.

I want to rush forward and kiss him.

Tell him I forgive him and...

... settle down, Kassidy.

I keep quiet, my lips plastered in a thin line, waiting for the apology to come.

He shakes his head and throws his arms across the doorway in a flamboyant fashion. "I fucked up. I'm a complete douchebag, and I don't deserve your friendship."

I allow a few seconds to pass before I agree. "All very good points."

Still yet to step inside the door, he looks forlorn and disappointed in himself. "Can I take you for breakfast before I head into the gallery, please?" Begging looks damn fine on him.

Part of me wants to draw this out, but I need a shower.

"Only if you're paying," I quip.

"Absolutely, I am."

"Get in here." Returning his smile, I direct him inside with a gentle nudge of my head. "Make yourself at home while I take a quick shower and change."

The door latches shut, and Jarett takes a seat at the dining table while I run the shower, wishing he was joining me.

"Jarett, I think we need to talk about..." my finger flashes between us as we finish up our English breakfast muffins loaded with bacon and hash browns, "... whatever this is, or isn't, between us."

Looking resigned, Jarett agrees.

"But first, talk to me about what happened last night."

"I overreacted. I'm very fond of you, and I tend to take on the role of protector with women in my close circle of friends. I didn't mean to imply that you couldn't look after yourself, Kassidy." Jarett stretches out his legs, accidentally kicking my foot with his. "Sorry."

I ignore the apology as I sip my second coffee of the morning.

"You're one of the strongest and smartest women I know. Besides that, I have no right sticking my nose in your business. Even if we are *together*, it would be wrong of me to influence you in any way with such things."

He gets it.

Without me saying a word, he knows he fucked up and isn't afraid to acknowledge it.

This is something I can appreciate and value in a man.

A man I'm quite sure I want more of.

"If I can say, and it's in no way justifying my behavior, but I was a little shocked Maxine would offer you a position like that. Usually, we discuss such matters, and especially since I introduced the both of you, it seemed a little out of place. But when Max sets her mind on something or someone, there's no holding her back."

I consider what he's saying. "Maxine will usually discuss staffing matters with you before making a decision?"

"Right, I guess that seems odd. First off, I dabble in a few businesses on the side, and I may have helped to finance the buy-in for the speakeasy in the beginning."

Now it makes sense. "Ahh, I get it. You're like a silent partner, then?"

"We don't refer to it that way. I invested in her business, and it's all hers. I wiped my hands of anything to do with the running and marketing side of it. Because we're family friends, I guess I've often been her sounding board for many things such as staff coming and going. As I said, it isn't an issue. I just got my jockstrap a little twisted in the wash, is all."

I laugh out loud at the visual.

"Maxine may have also reminded me that as the night went on, I was bitching like a little girl about men trying to get in the pants of gorgeous bartenders like yourself." He cringes, dragging his hand over his five o'clock shadow. "I'm embarrassed to say I may have been hit with the green-eyed monster, thinking of you meeting new people… guys, in particular, and them trying to take advantage of you."

Silently, I prompt him to continue. It improves my mood to know he was jealous.

"Truthfully, Kassidy, I trust you'd never let anybody, especially a drunk patron, take advantage of you, and God knows, I believe you can handle yourself."

My arms relax over my full stomach as I recline in my chair. "You're a great man, Jarett Evans. And thank you very much for explaining all this to me."

As much as I hate how he reacted, I understand why he did. What's more, I understand the thought processes which conjured up that type of reaction. While I'm a little perturbed by the outburst, it's also out of character from what I've come to know of him. Which isn't a big deal, I know, but Sophia and Maxine both assure me of the same thing.

"Now I've swallowed my pride and apologized, can I safely ask how your trial went yesterday?"

Yesterday was tough. Not the training or going to work on no sleep, but the part where I couldn't call Jarett when I finished up to tell him all about my day. I left my phone at home when I went to work and was gone almost twelve hours. When I returned home, I fell into bed in a heap, missing the numerous missed calls from Jarett until I woke for my run this morning.

"Firstly, I'm glad to hear how happy you are about me working at Maximum because you're looking at the newest addition." I shoot my arms out wide, seeking attention, and I get it.

He claps his hands together and takes a small bow in his seat. "Congratulations, my love. When is your first paid shift? Do I need to rearrange my schedule so I can be there to look out for you?"

The nerve.

I shoot daggers at him from across the table. He holds his hands up in defense. "Joking, love." He laughs, ducking to avoid the crumpled up napkin I throw at him. "I'm joking."

"Max isn't going to roster me on until after I have met with the new boss on Saturday. I should know more about what's expected, where I'll be working out of, that sort of thing."

"Are you nervous about the big meet and greet?"

"Nope, I'm excited. As a dedicated planner, I like to know all the details, which I'm noticeably light on at present, so I can't wait to get the full rundown. That way, I can plan other aspects of my life accordingly."

"Hmm? What other aspects would these be?"

"I like my time to be spent efficiently. I look forward to joining a gym and planning my classes around work, and then, of course, I can start at Maximum."

Jarett settles the check and helps me into my coat. I'm almost due to meet Sophia to find the most fabulous Gatsby creations for tomorrow evening.

With his hand on my back, we walk out of the diner. "Sounds like all that won't allow a lot of time for anything else, but as long as you'll be happy, I'm happy too." His smile doesn't quite reach his eyes.

We need to have that chat sooner than later.

Chapter 25

KASSIDY

I run my fingers over the beads of a peacock blue flapper gown to the fringe at the bottom. "This is beautiful."

Sophia pulls it from the rack of her go-to vintage boutique store and screws up her face. "Gorgeously elegant. It screams Kassidy, but not slutty enough by a long shot," she addresses me with a stern expression, placing it back on the rack and pulls me to a different section of the store.

"Not slutty enough? For whom?"

"Roaring twenties events are all around us. We can go to a flapper party any day of the week here in London. My birthday party…" she pauses, staring off into the distance for effect, "… it will be the sluttiest Gatsby-style event ever to hit this city."

Of course, it will.

"Okay, good to know. Can I ask what you are wearing?"

Her hand flies to her chest. "It's a surprise I can't reveal."

Rolling my eyes, she pulls a beaded lace corset from the rack with a deep, plunging neckline. Her eyes light up, and the oohs and aahs make it sound like she'll be screaming daddy's name in about two point five seconds.

Holding it up against my body, I'm shocked when she announces, "This is the one. Add an elegant headpiece, thick feather boa, and thigh-high garters. Don't give me that look," she adds pointedly. "I know you love to wear fishnets… you'll be comfortably you." She hands me the hanger and orders me to the change room.

I peruse the small but glamourous piece of fabric hanging in front of me. "Comfortably me? Sophia, I'll be practically naked."

"And perfectly slutty, my love. Try it on." She slams the door shut and leaves me to gawk at the costume in private. By God, if she's setting me up to wear this, and she walks in with an elegant ankle-length gown, I'll kill her.

"I can't hear you moving around in there." A light knock from the other side of the door flips me into action.

Standing in front of the mirror, I admire my perky breasts, loving the way they sit naturally with deep cleavage. *Damn, I look hot.*

"It's a perfect fit," I yell out. "But there's no way I'm walking out of here dressed in only this."

Sophia huffs from the other side, and her feet scurry across the floor away from me. I open the door to the changing room the slightest bit to peer around the shop searching for her. Suddenly, she appears with a garter, stockings, head and wrist piece.

I sigh. There's no way of getting out of this. She throws everything in a bundle into my hand and pulls the door closed.

A few minutes later, after fighting with the garter and trying to position the headpiece correctly without squeezing my brains out, a teal feather boa lands over the door scaring the shit out of me.

Sophia snickers when I yelp in fright. I wrap it behind my neck and rest it over the insides of both elbows as I've seen in the movies. I'm pleased with the additional pieces, no longer screaming naked and exposed. Instead, my self-confidence increases dramatically.

I step out of the stall, and Sophia spins around, her jaw flapping in the proverbial wind. "Holy sweet fuck, Kassidy. I'm going to need to rethink my outfit now. You're going to outshine me. You look fucking amazing."

I twirl for her, the only skin void of fabric are my arms, a few inches between my ass and the tops of my thighs where the stockings sit, and, of course, my neck through my chest and down to my torso where the deep plunge finally concedes.

"Slutty enough for you?" I ask, hands on my hips. "You better be wearing something equally revealing." I point my finger at her.

A devilish grin spreads over the face, "Oh, I am. I'll be showing off my body for the world to see. At forty, it may be the last time."

She's adamant about this, so I trust I'll not stand out poorly.

Hanging out with Sophia today was so much fun, and yet, I return home following our mani-pedi and facials homesick as fuck. I curl up on the sofa and FaceTime with my girls, who just happen to be together in the wee hours of Saturday morning.

The chat doesn't last long because none of them are talking any sense at all. Before I know it, tears flow from my eyes, cascading torrents of sadness.

I sniffle and wipe my eyes to steady the run, conscious of having my facial ruined by dark, puffy crying eyes.

Jarett is due here within the hour so we can discuss the fling or no-fling situation, but my heart feels too tender for any serious conversation right now. I call him instead of texting so he doesn't think I'm putting him off. He picks up after a few rings.

"Kassidy, need me to bring anything tonight? A bottle of wine?"

"I was hoping we could reschedule if you don't mind, I'm feeling a little off."

"Did something go awry with Sophia and the Botox bitches today?"

God, he makes me laugh. "Botox bitches?"

He laughs heartily on the other end of the phone. "What's the matter? I didn't poison you with a free breakfast this morning, did I?"

Tears well up and spring free again until I'm sobbing into the phone.

Fuck my life! What the hell is going on?

"Kassidy, are you crying, love?"

"I'm fine. Just a little homesick after the day with the girls. I'd rather curl up in bed."

The reception starts to fail. "Breaking up... hear you... ten minutes." And he's gone.

Fuck.

Assuming he's on the subway, reception is poor in the tunnels. Soon, he'll be knocking at the door, home to a blubbering mess who doesn't want any company.

I fiddle around with the costume items I bought

today and hang up the corset that cost me a small fortune. The doorbell soon jolts me from my self-pity party of one.

Shoulders back, I suck in a few deep breaths for good measure and open the door.

"Baby, are you okay?"

Good measure, my ass.

Salty tears stream down my cheeks and puddle in my hair tossed over my collarbone. Jarett places the shopping bag inside the door, pulls me to his chest, and slams the door shut with his foot.

Breaking our embrace after wetting his jacket with my tears, I assure him I'm fine, just a little homesick.

"Funny that, I have just the thing to cure homesickness." Bending over to collect the bag of goodies he brought with him, he pulls out a Mars bar because he knows it's my favorite chocolate, wine because I can't live without it, tissues because he's telepathic, and chopsticks.

Taking the tissues into the kitchen, he follows.

"Which part of your care package is just the thing for homesickness?"

"This may come as a surprise to you, but in my younger days when my parents were still alive, Sophia and I used to travel to Italy over the summer break to visit our aunt, my mum's sister. One year for whatever reason, Sophia couldn't go, but I insisted on going alone. I made it about ten days, living it up in a foreign country better than any other pre-teen I knew. Then snap, just like that..." he clicks his fingers, a faraway look in his eyes, "...reality set in, and I realized, although I wasn't alone, and I had visited multiple times before, I was missing home in a bad way."

I smile as Jarett recounts the memory wistfully. "My aunt held me all night that first night it hit, and I cried like a baby. Shhh..." he put his fingers to his lips, "... this doesn't leave this room."

I zip my lips shut and throw away the key.

"The next day my auntie made me pasta and cheesecake for dessert, my two favorite things, and let me open a prized bottle of grape juice, alcohol-free, of course, while we watched British movies and comedy shows all day. Before bed, I called home and slept like a grownup that night. No more tears."

My heart melted for the love this man shows me. Whatever kind of love it is, I want it. All of it.

Jarett is the most perfect best friend a girl could ever ask for.

"You knew I'd be on the brink of a meltdown when you saw me this morning, yet you said nothing?"

"This morning, you appeared to be perfectly intact. But the thought had crossed my mind which is why I was happy when you suggested we meet up tonight."

"After I left the gallery, I went out for supplies just in case." He shrugs as if it's the most normal part of any day.

"And if I'd not broken down on you?"

"No sweat, I'd have come up with another reason for having brought with me this outrageous array of items."

Without hesitation, I rush into his arms and stay there, allowing his warmth to embrace my vulnerabilities.

"Why the chopsticks?" I question into his shoulder.

"I wasn't sure about food items except for the Mars bar. I love to sit with a box of takeout noodles when I need to take a beat, so I thought we could order in some of the best noodles in England or whatever you desired."

"I love noodles."

Chapter 26

KASSIDY

The next thing I know, I'm stirring awake on the sofa, the lights are dim, and the credits are rolling on the television. We put on *The Sapphires*, Jarett's request, as his aunt had encouraged him to watch native movies to overcome the feeling of missing home. I've still never seen the end of that movie.

After dinner and a bottle of wine, I curled up on the sofa, my head on a cushion in Jarett's lap, and he covered me with a blanket, then I drifted off to sleep with him running his fingers softly up and down my back.

Sitting up, I realize I'm alone on the sofa. Across the room on the adjacent sofa, Jarett is sprawled out, legs over the end of the chair peeking out from beneath the other blanket. He's using his hands for a cushion because I greedily had them all stuffed under my head. Jarett must have given me another to compensate for him when he moved.

He looks uncomfortable yet peaceful, though I don't feel right leaving him there. I have one of the most important meetings of my life tomorrow, and I need a good night's sleep. From what I can tell, Jarett hasn't been sleeping the best this week either, so I hummed and hawed about waking him.

After brushing my teeth and turning off the television, I crouch beside him on the sofa, rubbing and gently shaking his shoulder. Movement behind his eyelids suggests he might wake if I continue to annoy him. I remove the blanket to find his long-sleeve shirt has ridden up and his lower torso, exquisitely defined, beckons me.

I lick my lips, remembering only last week, exploring this muscular terrain.

"Should I be scared?" His deep voice catapults me out of my seat.

I clutch my chest as it beats rapidly from the fright. "The fuck?"

Jarett swings his legs to the side. "You look as if you're ready to eat me."

He isn't wrong. I crave him like a crack whore chasing her next hit.

Instead of giving in and telling him he's right, I say goodnight and tell him I'm off to bed. Without moving, he raises his sleepy eyes to mine.

I hope Jarett will follow, but clearly, he needs me

to spell it out for him.

"Join me?"

With my meeting in the morning with Gabe Lugreno, a good night's sleep is essential. I can't risk lying awake thinking of Jarett on the sofa and all the delicious things I want to do to him. Knowing he'll be beside me will help me to get the best sleep.

That's the only reason.

Jarett narrows his eyes. "Are you sure you want that, Kassidy?"

Yes, I want it.

No, I'm not sure.

I am, but I know it's the last thing in the world I should be seeking right now.

Silently, I offer him my hand, and we go to bed.

We wake early from our deep slumber, and I bask in the glory of having Jarett's arm wrapped around me in a safe cocoon. The closer he snuggles behind me, the harder his erection pulses against me.

I don't want to move from this bed today, meeting or no meeting, until I've had all of him.

"Jarett?"

He moans behind me, the skin on the back of my neck prickling from the warmth of his breath. My fingers glide over the muscular edges of his forearm, silently begging him to touch me.

Jarett responds to my touch, tracing small circles across my tummy. Rolling over to face him, our lips are like magnets orbiting the same planet. Sucking on my bottom lip, then sweeping his tongue across it, I open to invite him in.

Our bodies entwine, moving together, drawing every satisfying touch from the other as our hands explore every crevice. I crawl over him until my clit is rubbing softly against his roaring erection.

"Kassidy, love, I need you so bad." Jarett groans into our kiss, and I respond in a soft, needy moan, "So much… I need you… too."

He peppers kisses across my throat.

"These past few days have been absolute fucking agonizing."

He grunts. "I don't want to be without you, Kassidy."

"Stop talking."

I raise myself slightly until I align with his cock. I grind my pussy over the head of his cock, coating myself in his pre-cum until I'm so fucking horny and close to coming, I need to stop, but I can't. When Jarett begins trembling beneath me, and I can't take it any longer, I lower myself until he's deep inside me.

"Ahh, fuck, woman. Your pussy feels so fucking good."

Our kiss deepens as I ride him, our bodies joined as one. Panting and moaning into each other's kiss, I continue to move above him, and he meets every movement with vigor. He flips me onto my back and hooks a leg over his forearm as he pushes himself deeper into my core. My fingers claw at his back. I'm so close.

So. Fucking. Close.

But I don't want it to end.

"Fucking hell, Kass—"

Jarett quickens his pace, his cock pulsing inside me, pushing me to the edge.

"Jarett, don't stop," I pant as he pulls my nipple between his teeth.

"Wait for me. I'm almost there, love."

Love.

Uncontrollably, I buck beneath him, our bodies slapping together in haste. My moans give out to a loud shriek, my orgasm rushing in as I feel him let go.

Jarett continues to move inside me, slowly, as we both linger in our post-orgasmic state. Moving me to his side so we're facing each other, Jarett caresses my cheek and kisses me tenderly.

"I've missed this so much," he whispers, his voice rough.

I run my hand over his shoulder and down his chest, committing every inch of his body to memory as if this might be our goodbye. "Me too."

A few moments pass as we lie in silence, soaking each other up. That's when I realize we didn't use a condom. Before I panic, my alarm beeps, and I bury deeper into the covers.

With my phone alarm buzzing incessantly on the side table, I'm due to get up and ready for my day ahead. I groan as I know I must pull myself away from Jarett despite him trying to keep me close.

And I love that he doesn't want to let me go.

Dressed and ready for business in the new English work attire that cost me more than a pretty penny this week, I enter the kitchen to find Jarett with a large mug of coffee ready and waiting.

Handing me the mug, Jarett peruses me from head to toe, his heated glare approving. "Fancy that, love. You scrub up damn nice for work too."

My cheeks blush from the compliment. It's an odd feeling to be preparing for work in a new country and meeting with a boss I haven't met even though he's already signed me.

"Are you nervous?" Jared asks as he sips his coffee.

"Not nervous, but I'm filled with jittery excitement. What if now that I've come to terms with London being my new home, we meet, and he decides I'm the wrong person for the job?"

"Hmm, I'd call those nerves, Kassidy. For the sake of it, though, how about we put it down to apprehension."

Yeah, I guess I'm apprehensive, but within the next few hours, I'll know for sure and have the direction I desire, so I can grasp my new life by the horns.

Chapter 27

KASSIDY

I arrive ten minutes early. The receptionist requests I take a seat and wait for Mr. Lugreno, who will be with me in a moment. The unfamiliar memories of my first job interview come to mind, and I wring my hands together in my lap.

The building is one of the largest in Central London and, thankfully, on my side of town. I could easily walk from my current apartment within fifteen minutes, but today, I take the subway which is only a two-minute walk from here. I don't want to risk being late for my first meeting, and the six minutes on the subway gives me a moment to collect myself in preparation.

The off-white with dark gray and black trim gives the building's interior a sleek and professional feel. The odd splash of color in the form of abstract prints and fake shrubbery enhance the ambiance, making it a little more inviting.

On the sign at the entrance, it shows Lugreno Enterprises is situated on the seventh floor, though the main receptionist insists I wait in the lobby for somebody to collect me and take me up, as security passes are required.

Taking my phone from my bag, I double-check it's set to silent.

"Kassidy?"

"Yes." My head twists in the direction of the female voice beside me. "Oh, I'm sorry, I didn't hear you approach," I tell her, downplaying the minor panic.

Her smile is wide and genuine. "My apologies. Mr. Lugreno is ready to meet with you now."

I collect my coat and secure my bag over my shoulder as I follow her down the hall and onto the first available elevator. She swipes her ID card and formally introduces herself.

"My name is Elise, I'm Mr. Lugreno's personal assistant. I travel with him to keep his schedule organized. For most things, I'll be your first point of contact as Mr. Lugreno is extremely busy and rarely available."

Good to know. I accept her dainty hand when offered. "Where's Mr. Lugreno based, so to speak?"

Elise offers a polite smile. "Mr. Lugreno will give you all the details you require in the meeting."

I offer a tight smile in return.

When we exit the elevator, I'm shocked to see a vastly different style of décor. There's a central reception desk which I assume is where Elise works, and not a thing is out of place. The walls are sparse, and the metal artwork is void of any color.

The white floors sparkle beneath the charcoal-colored walls, and there's not a thing on them except the office furniture. A large lobby area consists of vacant space void of personality with no chairs, sitting area, fancy décor, or splashes of color.

"Wait one moment, please."

Elise leaves me in the open space fitted with floor-to-ceiling windows overlooking London as she returns to her workstation and picks up her phone.

"Miss Moore is here," she directs into the phone.

A door springs open across the room as I'm sweeping the seven-story views above the city. Gabe Lugreno strides toward me, glaringly larger the closer he gets. Dressed in an over-the-top expensive dark gray suit, he is much younger than I imagined him to be.

My version of Mr. Grey in the flesh. Except for his shiny cobalt dress shirt, he's all but camouflaged in his office.

Taking a few steps toward him, I extend my hand.

"Miss Moore, what a pleasure to meet you in person," he drawls in a pronounced New York accent.

"Likewise, Mr. Lugreno."

"Please, call me Gabe, unless referring to me in conversation with a client or contractor. We'll spend too much time corresponding over the next twelve months to worry about formalities."

Got it. Gabe, it is.

He sweeps the open area with his hand. "I apologize for the bleak existence of the office. The head office is in New York as I'm sure you're aware, which is where I spend most of my time between commencements of new projects. I haven't had business in London for some time now and rented us this floor last week. My decorator will be in this evening and tomorrow to create my desired work effect," he assures me.

"Makes sense."

His gaze darts quickly in my direction, and he laughs.

"Please don't tell me you thought I enjoyed working in a cloud of darkness?"

I chuckle at his relaxed temperament, happy to say I got him all wrong. "Of course not. Elise advised she travels with you wherever you go, so I take it you have no permanent staff here."

"Correct. Walk with me." He waves in the direction of the elevators. "I wanted to meet you here, so you know where our base is, but I'd prefer to discuss matters over a drink and some tapas. Is that okay with you?"

"Absolutely."

Retracing my steps from earlier, Gabe elaborates on my previous question. "I work mostly with contractors, and my clients rarely come to me. I'm hands-on and prefer to meet with my people where it suits them best."

I remain quiet, listening intently.

"All written correspondence between the both of us will be seen by Elise, of course, and she only comes to me if she needs clarification. Otherwise, she answers on my behalf. Her responses are gospel, and she knows me better than myself."

He glances across at me as we walk in the opposite direction to the way I arrived. "You may speak freely, Kassidy. Jump in with questions as you wish. This is a very informal meet-and-greet so we have the chance to get to know each other. "

"Thank you."

"I arrived on the red-eye last night," Gabe continues. "Initially, my trip was to be for personal reasons only. I have a birthday event to attend this evening, and then you showed up on my radar. Would you believe?"

Call me curious.

"May I ask how I showed up on your radar?"

"It was an odd chain of events." We stop out front

of a downtown restaurant, and Gabe directs me inside. A waiter ushers us to a table for two by the window—only a few tables are occupied being on the earlier side of the lunch rush. Taking a seat, Gabe orders a bottle of water for the table and a bottle of sauvignon blanc.

"The party I'm attending tonight has been on my schedule for months now, and I've been to and fro with a new client over the past year. He has been negotiating on the acquisition of several hotels currently operating in some warehouse space on the outskirts of London. His dream is to turn them into a new hotel chain. It was only last week that the contracts went through for these acquisitions, and we've been talking for a couple of months about the vision he had for these bars and clubs."

Gabe takes a breath to sip his water when the waiter appears. I continue scribbling at rocket speed in my notebook.

"He's been leaning toward incorporating an Australian feel to some of them because we have many ex-pats here in London, and he thinks it would be good business sense to bring the locals a mixture of culture. With the contracts confirmed and approved, I then wait for him to hand over the acquisitions for me to work with contractors like yourself and plenty of others in different areas to put his vision into reality."

I nod quietly, focused on the chain of command.

"Upon the finalization, I took to investigating designers and digital creators with an interest and vast experience in the design of clubs and hotels. In doing so, I happened upon the name of a corporation in Australia and made a call on a Sunday, thinking I'd hit a message bank and be expecting a call back later in the week.

However, I guess it's true that some Aussies work twenty-four seven as we do, and your boss, Malcolm, answered after the first few rings. I had looked over your profile on the website before calling him."

A different waiter returns with the bottle of wine and proceeds to pour for the both of us. I'm completely intrigued and desperate to know what had led Gabe Lugreno to me. But so far, it seems like my stars aligned, and here I am.

"So..." he continues, "... imagine my surprise when Malcolm tells me that his very own superstar was currently vacationing in this wonderful city. I didn't want to risk you going home and choosing not to return, so I opted to set up a meeting with you as soon as humanly possible, which is today."

"Well, that's some chain of events. Thank you for the opportunity."

He nods, passing me a glass which I happily receive.

"I do require all my contractors and subcontractors to be hands-on because I feel if they are walking in and out of our competitors' bars and lounges regularly, they are carrying around the inspiration they need to truly manufacture the vision that my client has for his hotel chains. Therefore, I usually seek a local contractor, but needing expertise specifically from an Australian who also knows the ins and outs of the hotel industry, I had to look abroad for this project."

"And I'm grateful."

Gabe is all business, not one for small talk.

"My only dilemma, however, is we're in the process of this work being transferred over to me. As in, I'll have full run of these acquisitions based on my client's wishes. This effectively will not be done for at least a couple of weeks yet, but I needed to secure you when I could. Hence, why I agreed to put you up in one of the best apartment blocks in Shoreditch, which is over and above the general contract rate."

I stop scribbling. "So, you're saying I won't be starting on this job effective immediately?"

Those jitterbugs swarming my tummy earlier today are back in full flight, their wings stronger than ever.

"Yes and no. The fact is, I want to wrap up this part of the project within twelve months, as discussed. You can get started on the design brief, and there are many places I'd like you to visit over their busiest periods to engage in some blind surveys and muster up appropriate feedback… what people are looking for, etcetera, and including some competitor and market research without exposing who you work for or the task at hand, of course."

My face lights up. "You want me to go deep undercover, a rogue agent even?"

Gabe laughs, and again, all is well in my world.

"I'll keep you busy with questions, discovery briefs, design manipulation processes, and all the works while you're frequently coming to me with your new ideas and design concepts of your own. I imagine everything will be fully planned and documented with necessary contractors and staff in place to carry out the refurbs within three months. That's when we'll begin working more closely with the corporate owner."

"Sounds perfect. I thrive on being kept busy. Researching pubs, clubs, and restaurants is right up my alley too."

"Oh, I've heard, and from your portfolios, you have a real knack for it."

While we enjoy our lunch, we discuss the apartment which is ready for me to move into tomorrow and the company credit card I now have for any food, drinks, or entertainment expenses while conducting required research and, of course, any other business-related expenses.

"One more thing I must hand over to you is your

retainer check."

Cha-ching, dollar signs invade my line of sight.

"Oh yes, that's very generous of you. It will be put to good use, I assure you."

Gabe reminds me that these funds are for travel back home should I wish to take the trip before I commence work on these initial stages and anything I require to set up my new abode.

If you can email Elise your banking details, the transfer to your account will be made immediately.

"Thank you again, and I have decided to wait until further into the year when there's an opportunity for a break to visit home. I'm worried if I go now, it will be difficult to return."

Gabe stares at me intentionally before he adds, "You're a wise woman, Kassidy."

Chapter 28

KASSIDY

After we polish off the last of the wine, Gabe excuses himself to the restroom. During lunch. I noticed my phone buzzing silently in my bag at my side. I expect to find exciting texts from Sophia about tonight, but no, it's Jarett who's been blowing up my phone, checking on my progress and ETA back home.

> **Jarett**: *Let me know when you're done. I'm at the gallery, we can head home together.*
> **Jarett**: *Sorry. That's if you want to.*
> **Jarett**: *No pressure.*
> **Jarett**: *Assume you're still in your meeting, hope it's going well.*
> **Jarett**: *About tonight, I want to ask you*

something but not sure if I should.
Jarett: *Text me when you get this.*

I smile at the barrage of texts, and instantly, I'm intrigued by what he wants to ask me tonight.

Quickly, I tap out a response.

Jarett: *Finishing up lunch, the boss down the street from the gallery. I'll stop by when done? And you should. Ask me... I think.*

"If there's nothing more you wish to discuss today, Kassidy, I think we should finish up and get on with our weekend. Would you agree?"

"Absolutely. Just one thing. Do you want me to report to the office each day and work from there or—"

"Not at all, the office is for appearance only. If you stop by on Monday morning, say nine o'clock, you can check out the new digs and your office before Elise and I fly back to New York at noon. For the most part, I assume you'd rather work remotely. The apartment has a huge office set up and taps directly into our server in New York."

Of course, every single detail has been planned and executed perfectly.

"Okay then, I have no further questions at this time but know where to reach you if I do."

Gabe shakes my hand and ushers me out the door of the restaurant, him peeling off in one direction while I head straight for the gallery.

"Please ask me before I overthink it and assume the worst," I state boldly as I walk into Jarett's office.

"Hello, love. Nice to see you. How was your meeting? My day has been wonderfully productive, thank you for asking," he answers sarcastically with a smartass smirk.

I flop into the chair opposite his desk, where he's elbows deep in paperwork. "I'm sorry. You, too, the meeting was great, yay for productivity, and you're welcome," I shoot back, with a cheeky poke of the tongue.

Clearly impressing him with my wit, I can't help but chuckle. These British men think they're all over the sarcasm, but this one has never messed with an Aussie girl before.

Jarett rounds his desk and lowers his ass on the edge, his legs hip-width apart on either side of the chair I'm sitting on.

"I promise my question isn't awful, unless, of course, your answer is no."

Not a fan of riddles.

"Hit me with it, and we'll see what the damage is."

Jarett throws his head back, and I admire his throat and the dark stubble as it grazed the inside of my thighs earlier this morning.

"Hmm?"

Dammit. Caught daydreaming.

"Even a no would be better than stone-dead silence. Geez."

Laughing, I apologize for my absentmindedness.

"I'd like to take you to my sister's party tonight... as my date," he pushes out hesitantly.

"Oh." I chastise myself for all the things I thought he might have been going to say. "Of course," I respond, frowning slightly. "Why would you worry about asking me that?"

He leans into me, his hands on the arms of the chair. "Our five-night fling is over. You've made that clear. What isn't clear to me is what we are now."

I gulp, my brain a foggy mess with Jarett so close. "I don't know. What are we?" The words escape in a whisper.

Jarett lowers his face to my neck, his tongue flicking out, running upward to my ear. Teasing my earlobe with his teeth, my body seethes beneath him.

"What do you want, Kassidy?" he whispers in my ear.

I don't know.

I'm terrified to admit the truth to myself.

I want him.

I know I do.

More than I've wanted for anything.

For the first time in my life, I want more than a successful career.

I want someone worthy of sharing it with.

But not just *someone*.

Jarett.

Jarett kisses his way across my jaw until his breathing mixes with mine, and his mouth hovers over my lips, waiting for me to speak.

"I want you, Jarett. I *need* you."

Our lips collide, his arms weave around my back, and he lifts me from the chair. Desperation takes over, and clothes are torn from each other in an unorganized manner. I step out of my skirt and yank down the zipper of his jeans.

Almost naked, he turns me toward the desk and pushes me forward. One hand in my hair, he anchors himself to me while he uses his spare hand to pull my lace thong to the side. His jeans fall to the floor behind me, and instantly, his cock is at my entrance.

I'm soaking wet, rubbing myself up and over him. He drives into me, deep and purposefully.

Claiming me.

Marking me.

Working up to a steady rhythm, he pumps inside me, the top half of my body over the desk. The friction of my lace bra on my nipples as I slide over the desk again and again is hardening my nipples and turning me on even more.

Jarett reaches over me, taking both my hands and pulls them toward him. Holding them in position over my lower back, he changes his angle and slaps my ass.

Hard.

A yelp escapes, and a groan follows as he rubs the area where his palm connects.

Another slap. Harder again on the other cheek.

This time I squeal.

"Quiet."

I grit my teeth and ride the pleasure train to Mount O.

Twice.

Chapter 29

KASSIDY

The doorbell chimes.

I'm flushed from cramming into my corset and garter stockings after I styled my hair and painted my face. I've mastered the porcelain and oh-so twenties look.

"Coming," I yell, unsure how soundproof these walls are.

Racing down the hall to the front door, I pause, taking a moment to center myself. Inhaling deeply, I run my hands down my corset.

I open the door and stand against it, pin-up style.

Jarett's mouth falls open, and his facial features darken as he soaks up my outfit, perusing my body like a starved predator.

"Kassidy, holy fuck." His words fall from his lips in a coarse whisper.

Gangster Jarett is hot as fuck too. He wears those suspenders and top hat like a boss.

I swing my arm out, inviting him in. He stumbles through the door, lost for words.

"You're looking dapper yourself," I purr, closing the door behind us. When I turn, Jarett is staring at my legs. Specifically, my exposed thighs between where the fishnet stockings end and my corset begins.

Instantly, I twitch, standing uneasy on my heels.
Exposed and insecure.

He drags his gaze to my face and must see my internal agony.

"Sweetheart, you look hot as fucking hell." He runs his fingers over his chin as if contemplating what to say next.

"But?"

Jarett hesitates a moment before shaking his head. "But nothing. You're so fucking sexy, I'm speechless."

I eye him curiously before I explain it is Sophia's wish for all the women to wear slutty over elegant costumes.

"Ah." He nods, his lips forming in a straight line. "Of course, she did."

I give him a raised-eyebrow quizzical look to which he responds with a shrug. "That's my sister for you."

He forces out a laugh, but it's uneasy.

"If you're embarrassed to accompany me wearing this costume, Jarett, say it now, and we won't be seen together."

"What? No. I'm not letting you out of my sight dressed like that. I don't want men drooling over my woman."

I smile. "Your woman, huh?"

"That's what I said, sweetheart."

"One minute," I say, pointing a finger at him. Retreating to my bedroom, I fetch my teal feather boa to complete the look. One last look in the mirror, I pucker and smack my red-hot lips together.

Flicking off the lights, we're ready for the night to begin.

We enter the speakeasy together on what feels like our first official date as a couple. Secured to Jarett's arm, I peruse the room full of guests, looking for the lady of the evening. The décor is epic, every bit of what you'd expect for a roaring twenties party. Centerpieces grace every table, and a photo booth is set up in the corner opposite the band.

Guests mill around talking, laughing, and sipping on drinks of all kinds, mixes that can only be found here at Max's bar. Her mixology and creativity are inspiring. She brought in extra staff tonight to help as she's here as a guest. Though, I'm not surprised when I spot her pouring drinks behind the bar.

Roman is sitting on the opposite side watching her intently.

Jarett guides us through the crowd. "Where's the lady of honor?" he asks, pulling out two seats beside his brother.

"Planning her grand entrance, of course," Max answers with a smile and playful eye roll.

"I was under the impression you were a guest, not bar staff tonight, Max," Jarett states.

Roman jumps in. "Exactly what I was just saying but women…" he huffs, "… they never listen."

"No, you didn't just lump all us women together in that statement, Mr. Evans," I chide.

Roman laughs and pecks me on the cheek. His eyes wander respectfully over my body. "Damn, Kassidy, the twenties look good on you."

"Don't start," Jarett warns, and we all laugh.

The music lulls as we're finishing our first drink, and still, we haven't seen Sophia. Finger treats are being passed around on trays by waiters dressed in matching black and white gangster outfits, followed by a waitress in matching barely-there flapper dresses dispensing glasses of champagne to all the guests.

"We ask that everyone please get themselves a glass of bubbly in preparation for the birthday toast upon the arrival of Lady Sophia," the MC announces over the microphone from the stage.

Roman and Jarett both groan at either side of me.

"Classic Sophia." Jarett laughs, and I poke him with a scowl to keep him quiet.

Music commences again, a classic introduction, and the lights dim throughout, except for those in the stairs, and a huge chandelier lights up the bottom of the stairs waiting for Sophia to arrive.

As the music peters out to soft background noise, the crowd gasps, oohing and aahing as Sophia descends the stairs. With a man on her arm, his head is down, attention on the stairs as he guides Sophia safely to her party.

She's decadently dressed as a twenties whore. No doubt the exact look she's going for—her brown locks pinned back in a bob, a head of jewels, and long satin gloves adorning her slender arms. A sequin-covered gold corset pinches at her waist, boosting her voluptuous curves while her girls bust perfectly out the top. She's all class and all legs with strings of pearls falling daintily from the bottom of her corset.

"Who's the dude?" Roman queries.

"Not a clue, but I think we should take him out back and suss him out." Jarett is very fond of his sister and outrageously protective. Roman nods in agreement.

Poor Sophia. She has no hope of keeping a man in her life with these two fools around.

The couple in question steps into the limelight, and that's when the man on her arm raises his head and removes his hat.

What. The. Fuck.

"Presenting to you, Ms. Sophia Evans accompanied this evening by Mr. Gabe Lugreno. Please raise your glasses for a toast. Happy birthday, Lady Sophia, and congratulations on forty fabulous years. May the next forty be equally as brilliant."

No, it can't be.

"You can't be fucking serious." Jarett spits dirt beside me.

I snap my head toward him with a frown and whisper, "Do you know him?"

His eyes never leave Sophia and Gabe as he gulps his full beer in three goes. "You could say that."

A dreaded unease falls over me. "Jarett, that's my new boss."

"I know."

Chapter 30

KASSIDY

"What? How do you know?" I rack my brain trying to remember if I mentioned his name during any of our conversations, but I don't believe I did.

"Jarett?" I persist.

"I'll explain later, I promise." Jarett wraps his hand around mine and pulls me from my seat. "First, let's welcome Sophia and wish her a happy birthday."

I allow Jarett to direct me to Sophia and Gabe, my new boss. Confusion and the answers to the questions I have swirling around my head take a back seat. This is Sophia's special moment and be fucked if I'm going to ruin it for her.

"Sis, you radiate beauty. Happy fortieth." Jarett kisses his sister on the cheek and whispers something in her ear only she can hear. The glimpse of a scowl hidden beneath her radiant smile and hard stare tells me it wasn't a welcome comment.

I hustle my way in, breaking the tension between them. "Damn, woman, you're one hot fucking forty-year-old!" I swoon, kissing both her cheeks and hugging her to my chest.

"I'm so excited you could be here, it's the best birthday gift I could ask for. And this is—" She waves her hand to her left.

"Yes!" I step forward to offer my hand appropriately. "Mr. Gabe Lugreno, my new boss," I interrupt, shooting an awkward smile his way.

Jarett is less than thrilled.

Tension is rolling off both men.

What the fuck is going on?

Sophia's eyes bulge in shock. "Are you fucking kidding me?"

Feeling uncomfortably dressed in a corset standing in front of my new boss, I tell myself stranger things have happened. All four of us stand rigid, unsure where to look.

"What a surprise," I offer Gabe.

"Very much so," he answers, his attention flicking between the three of us.

Jarett excuses us so other guests can welcome Sophia. Roman catches up as we order another drink from the bar. I'm not a champagne-type girl, so I ditch that baby immediately once the toast is done.

"Did I miss something? Who is that guy with Sophia that you both seem to know?"

"My boss." I cringe, and Roman frowns, cocking his head at Jarett.

"My business partner and Sophia's fly-in hookup when he's here on business."

Oh my God. This city is closing in on me, a new meaning to *it's a small world*.

I chug down a few mouthfuls of my margarita, opting for a more basic drink tonight so I one, don't bust the seams on my corset, and two, avoid making a drunken fool of myself in front of the mystery guy paying my excessive wage and putting me up in a gorgeous apartment.

Jarett and Roman are discussing the ins and outs of the business partnership, and I pretend not to listen. Hard, considering I'm standing between them. For the first few seconds at least, I hold up the façade.

"You buy the property and present it to Gabe with a business plan or idea?"

Jarett avoids eye contact with me. "As simple as that, yes."

"And he manages the development and design of your idea to bring it to fruition?"

My heart beats more rapidly. I'm unsure if it's the anticipation of his answers, the tequila working through my veins, or the sinister idea he created a job for me, so I'd stay in the country.

Jarett parks his beer on the bar with a louder-than-necessary thump and glares at me. "That's how it works, Kassidy. You should know this. You work for him."

"Whoa, why are you being such a dick, man?" Roman interrupts.

Jarett's stare remains hard and focused on me. Confusion fades to understanding.

"No. Uh-uh. It can't be." I shake my head in slow motion, afraid to look away from him in case he gives me a sign I'm thinking along the wrong lines.

"Jarett, is it one of your investments I'm hired to work on?" My body temperature rises, sweat beads beneath my stockings, and the skin on my arms where the boa rests begins to irritate me.

"Mind if I join?" All three of us snap our heads in the direction of the voice.

Gabe Lugreno.

"Please do," I welcome him, and he stands on the other side of Jarett.

"Jarett was just explaining to me how you two know each other. You know, because it's a tad strange that we're dating…" I point between Jarett and myself, "… and now I'm working for his developer in a foreign country. Don't you think?"

"On that note, I'm off to mingle with the sexy singles of the party," Roman cuts in. "Good luck, bro."

He's going to need more than luck to navigate

the shit fight brewing in my head. Trust me.

Gabe, on the other hand, appears genuinely surprised. "Now that is strange. You know..." he adds, mirroring my earlier response, his eyes darting between us, "... because when Jarett contacted me about hiring you—"

I slam my cocktail glass on the bar and face Jarett, my hand on my hip and fury in my eyes. His head falls back in defeat, though he remains neutral, avoiding eye contact with either of us.

"I didn't realize you were dating," Gabe finishes, looking confused by my outburst.

"We weren't," Jarett interjects at the same time as I answer, "We aren't."

Gabe uses this moment to excuse himself from the situation entirely. "Looks like you two could use a moment to catch up on some details. Sorry, J." He pats Jarett's shoulder and strides off.

"What did you do, Jarett? Explain. Right now."

My patience is shattered, my new life in London appears to be balancing on an unstable mountain of deceit, and I demand to know what the fuck is going on right this minute.

"Max's office. Please?" He extends his hand to me, but I whisk around and storm off through the staff area at the back of the club, refusing to give him the satisfaction of being a united front on this.

Sophia is stepping out of the bathroom as we make our way to the offices. "You two off for a quickie already? The night's only young." She laughs, hugging us both in the hall, blocking our escape.

"Not exactly," I pout. "Your brother appears to have manipulated my position with your friend, Gabe, and in doing so, has turned my world upside down. And I'm about to find out why."

Sophia steps back from us and glares silently at Jarett. "No, you didn't, baby bro," she chastises.

Jarett huffs. "If I can have a minute with Kassidy to explain, you can all calm the fuck down."

Calm the fuck down?

My blood reaches boiling point, and I sneer at him with warning.

The bastard has the gall to roll his eyes at me.

Sophia removes herself from our path and pushes us further down the hall. "Get this mess sorted, Jarett. It's my birthday for fuck's sake. We're supposed to be partying."

She's right, and I feel awful that I'm wasting the night this way, but I must know what led to me getting offered this job.

In Max's office, I take her chair behind the desk, and Jarett plants his ass on the edge of the desk in front of me. Waiting for him to explain his life away, I nervously twirl the boa around my fingers.

"It's not what you think, Kassidy."

"Great, and what is it that I'm thinking?"

"I never asked any favors of Gabe. You have to

believe me."

Huh.

"I'll be the judge of that. Explain what happened. Gabe said he was referred by someone to my firm and found out I was in London after he spoke to my boss, Malcolm."

"Partially true." He removes his gangster hat and runs his hands along his thighs.

"I mentioned your firm in Australia, told Gabe I met you here in London, and you were only here a few days. I told him I believed you could bring a lot of value to the project because I do."

"So, you wanted *me*, specifically, to work on the design and roll-out of this project for *you*? Pubs and clubs with a British Aussie feel? Because of my experience and nothing to do with the fact we were sleeping together."

"Yes." He answers immediately.

I launch to my feet and wander about Max's office for a few seconds. "Then why the fuck, Jarett? Why wouldn't you talk to me about it personally rather than go behind my back?"

"I didn't go behind your back, Kassidy. Well, not exactly."

I pin him with a pointed stare.

Not exactly?

Hmm.

"Okay, I went to Gabe about you, and I should've spoken to you about it first. I'm sorry. I didn't think you'd be interested in the work if you knew I had something to do with it."

My face twists up at his stupidity.

Fucking men.

"How well did that turn out for you? I know about it now, after I've already signed the contracts, but it doesn't change the fact I'm still working for you and had no choice in the matter."

I brace myself on the opposite side of the desk and hang my head between my outstretched arms.

Breathe, Kassidy.

"I work with Gabe on this project, and he has hired you to do the work he has signed off on. You and I won't be working together."

"Right, so you banked on me never knowing that you set this job up for me. That you had nothing to do with moving my entire life from Australia to London for a whole fucking year?"

Jarett moves to sit on Max's chair as I take a seat in the visitor's chair across from him.

"I'm sorry, Kassidy, clearly I didn't think this through. I saw potential in having your knowledge and experience, your skillset associated with my project. I made a call to Gabe and made my case. He took it from there. No ultimatums, no secrets."

"So, this is purely professional?"

Sitting forward in his chair, his elbows rest on his thighs with his hands squeezed together, avoiding the question.

Motherfucker.

I want him to want me for more than a job. On the other hand, I'm pissed he used a job offer to keep me here to explore our relationship instead of fucking talking to me about it.

"Tell me it's nothing personal, Jarett. That this idea isn't concocted as some feasible way to keep me in London."

He winces and repeats my words back at me. Then he stops.

"I'm sorry, I can't." He shakes his head and slams his back into the chair, his arms behind his head, ankles crossed over his knee.

Fuck him looking so damn hot right now.

"Meaning?"

When his eyes find mine again, he looks defeated.

Sad.

Broken.

"I don't know. I just can't."

"Can't what, Jarett?" I ask softly.

What's he saying?

"I need to get back to the party," is all he offers as he walks past me and out the door, leaving me heartbroken and confused.

After fifteen minutes of sitting in solitude and visiting the ladies' room, I return to the party searching for Maxine. I spot Roman and Jarett in the corner by the bar talking to a couple of other guys I don't know.

Hell, I barely know anyone. I'm a stranger in a city far from my own, with a career opportunity I no longer know if I want.

I stay for at least another hour, doing the rounds with Max, meeting some of the guests, a fake smile plastered on my face. I drink margaritas like nobody is watching and dance my ass off with the birthday girl.

I did my part.

It's important to me not to let Sophia know how broken I am inside. There will be time to deal with all that tomorrow and the day after.

I hope.

Chapter 31

JARETT

When I need them the most, words escape me.

It's not the time or place to discuss us or our future, but I could've said something other than, *I can't*. It was the perfect opportunity to tell her how I feel.

What the fuck was I thinking?

Lying in bed alone at lunchtime on Sunday, I wonder if it's too early to call Sophia for some advice on what a dick I've been.

My phone remains completely silent since Kassidy's text last night to say she made it home safely and needs some time alone to think. If I hadn't seen her leave and called to check on her, I probably wouldn't have heard from her at all.

Why would I?

"Jarett Christopher Evans, where the fuck are you?"

Ugh.

I need to take my key from her.

I climb unwillingly out of bed and throw on a pair of sweatpants to deal with my sister. And beg for her best advice.

"You look terrible," I report, walking into the living room. "Big night?" I smirk.

"No worse than you, little bro, except I happened to have a ridiculously fantastic night and even better sex this morning."

I raise my palm. "Please, stop. Too much information."

"Don't you want to know why I'm here?" she screeches, taking a seat at the breakfast bar.

"Nope. Guessed that all on my own," I answer, pulling two bottles of water from the refrigerator.

"Kassidy filled me in. What are you going to do to fix this mess?"

"What can I do?" I shrug. "I fucked up, I apologized. I understand how she feels, but I never intended anything in the way she's interpreted it."

"Of course, you didn't. You're just a thirty-six-year-old man child with no fucking idea of how women think. Why would you need to?" Her eyes roll back in her head with exaggerated effort.

"What do you want me to say, Sophia? I've no clue how to navigate this."

"You didn't want her to leave, so you preyed on her career advancement goals to keep her here."

"Geez, hit me where it hurts and tell me what you think, why don't ya?"

"Is it true, Jarett? Because that's how I see it. But Kassidy, she's confused. Thinking you did it for her career only, and you've ended things with her because she found out you went behind her back to get her a job she didn't ask for, instead of talking to her like an adult."

"Wait, she thinks I ended things with her?"

Sophia stares at me blankly. "Something about you muttering the words, *I'm sorry, I can't do this*, and walking out. Ring a damn bell?"

I bury my face in my hands. A royal fucktastrophe, that's what this is.

"That's not what I meant, for fuck's sake." I groan into my palms.

"Hmm, I figured. Kassidy, on the other hand..."

I fold my arms on the counter and wait for the big sister's advice to start flowing.

"You love her." It's a statement, not a question, and it throws me off guard.

"I've known her for five damn minutes."

"And loved her for three hundred seconds."

Fuck.

"I was her holiday fling. I can't tell her that."

"Well, she's not on holiday anymore, thanks to you. And I never, in your five years of marriage or before, ever saw you look at Helena the way you look at Kassidy."

Sucker punch received.

"So, what do I do, ol' wise one of forty years?"

Sophia jumps from her stool and throws her hands in the air. "I thought you'd never ask. Go to her. Now." She hands me her phone, unlocking it to show me a message.

"Nope, she asked for space, and I have to respect that."

"My ass you do, look at this." Sophia points to a thread of messages between herself and Kassidy. The last being a screenshot of a plane ticket.

For Kassidy.

Destination—Australia.

Tonight.

"Oh fuck no." My feet land on the tiles before my mind has a chance to catch up. I shower and dress in record time and race out the door with Sophia on my heels.

"You can go now, thank you," I scowl at her as we exit the elevator on the ground level.

"And risk you fucking this up for good? Not today, bro. Not today."

Sophia always has a way of having my back but also making me feel ten years old again. There's no getting out of this one, though.

She loves Kassidy too.

Ten minutes later, I'm banging on her door louder than usual.

"Who is it?"

I point at Sophia, prompting her to answer for me. Kassidy will be more likely to answer the door for her.

"It's Sophia. Open up, woman."

Moments pass, which feel like minutes drowning in quicksand.

The door opens, and Kassidy stands there, wrapped in a towel with her hair in rollers. She's fucking adorable.

Her gaze dances between the two of us before she pops her head outside the door, looking up and down the corridor.

"Quick, come in before my nosey neighbor sees me inviting guests in, while sporting this hot mess attire."

One hell of a hot mess.

The women exchange kisses when we're safely inside. I, however, am afforded a what-the-fuck-are-you-doing-here glance.

"He's my brother, Kassidy. I had to tell him."

Kassidy sighs.

"I didn't want any goodbyes, Soph."

"Then don't go, Kassidy. Please." I've never had the desire to grovel at a woman's feet as much as I do right now.

I follow her to the sofa and sit across from her,

careful not to invade her space more than I already have.

"Firstly, I didn't need my sister to show up today to inform me of what a massive jerk I was last night. When I said, *I can't,* I didn't mean I can't do us, I was referring to the words I needed to say but couldn't."

"Jarett, despite what you couldn't say last night, my life changed the day I met you. For the better. Days later, I'm no longer a visitor but a permanent resident for twelve months, both an exciting and daunting prospect." She stands and paces around the room.

Sitting, watching her in a state of confusion kills me.

"When I thought I'd been contracted for this project based on my professional merits, it was a dream come true. Now, I feel like a fraud—"

"It's not—" My words halt as she casts an evil stare my way.

"Please, Jarett, you came to me. Let me say what I need to."

I nod, urging her to continue.

"I feel less than deserving because a guy I was seeing for five fucking days had a hand in it and more than that, I feel betrayed. I'm hurt that you went about this without even discussing it with me."

"I get that now. I do. It never crossed my mind when I spoke with Gabe that it could be construed this way. Please, Kassidy, forgive me for being so short-sighted."

"I'm not one to hold grudges, Jarett. I think I need some time away from here to understand where I fit in based on my own merits and choices."

I nod solemnly.

Her words cut me deep. I've made her feel as if she doesn't deserve this, and it couldn't be further from the truth.

Sophia stands off to the side, near the kitchen, giving us room to speak but listening to every word. When I glance up at her, she prompts me to keep talking.

"Look, Kass, for the most part, you're a perfect fit for the job. It's why the idea came to me in the first place. The opportunity, being contracted by the likes of the Lugrenos is a secure fast-track to career success, and I know that's important to you. But that was the second reason I went to Gabe."

I take a deep breath and focus my attention on the beautiful woman in front of me.

She rolls her hand at me, much like Sophia had, urging me to continue.

"You're important to me, Kassidy. In such a short time, you've become such a large part of my life. The most enjoyable part." I sigh in frustration. *Why can't I tap into my feminine side when I need to air my feelings.* "A part I never want to live without."

A tear runs down her cheek.

I want to move closer to her and wipe away her tears.

Kiss her lips.

Assure her I never meant to hurt her.

Never would I dream of taking away her ability to decide for herself. She's too strong a woman for that. And I love that about her.

Yet, without realizing it, that's exactly what I did.

"I might have been your five-night holiday fling, Kassidy, but during that time, you became my forever fling."

A small smile creeps across her face, and it encourages me to keep going. This may be my last chance to see her face to face. "Sophia was right when she said I didn't want to say goodbye to you." I shake my head, disgusted at myself. "Maybe I did use your career focus to engage you to stay, but I don't believe I did it maliciously. Consciously, I wasn't aware that's what I was doing."

Kassidy moves from the sofa to perch herself across my lap. She wraps her arms around my neck. Her head burrows into my chest, and slowly, my heart rate begins to even out.

"I believe you, Jarett."

She pulls away, smiles at Sophia, and kisses me softly.

"But I still have a plane to catch."

The actual fuck?

I want to scream at her, *you're still leaving.* But

the words die in my throat.

My heart hangs heavy in my chest. This feeling, it's the reason I never pined for human connection. The reason I avoid any form of meaningful relationships with women.

Sophia marches into the living room. "You're still leaving? As stupid as he was, Jarett declares his love for you, and you're going home to Australia without giving him a second chance?"

Whoa.

"Sophia," I warn.

I'm impressed Sophia is quick to jump to my defense, but seriously, I'm a grown-fucking-man.

Kassidy bursts out laughing. She scrambles from my lap, tears of laughter streaming down her face.

Did I miss something?

Sophia joins her in a fit of laughter, and I soon follow. These bitches are fucking *crazy*.

The moment passes, and Kassidy wipes the tears from her face. "I love you, Sophia," she cries, standing to hug my sister, who squeezes her back.

"Does that mean you'll stay?" she asks, full of hope.

Kassidy shakes her head, smiling. "I'm going home for a week to tie up a few loose ends and get grounded again."

Thank fuck. She's coming back to me.

Best. News. Ever.

"You're coming back." Sophia cries happily.

"I always was. I have a contract for the next twelve months, remember?"

Kassidy eyes me seriously. "I may have landed this job because of you, but I'm going to kick ass all over London and earn this position for myself."

This woman has lady balls, and I fall more in love with her every minute I'm in her presence.

"That's where you're wrong, Kass," I tell her honestly. "Lugreno offered you the job based solely on your portfolio. The success is all yours. He had no idea about our relationship."

Another smile spreads across her face and lights up her tear-filled eyes. "Thank you, Jarett. It means a lot."

"Come here." I stand for an embrace. My grip tightens around her body, not wanting to let her go. But one week without Kassidy won't kill me.

I hope.

What I'd never be able to deal with is a lifetime without her.

"What about us, Kassidy? When you return, where does this leave us?" I have to know before she leaves what's in store when she returns.

"Yes, Jarett. We're good."

Kassidy takes my face in her hands and kisses me.

Hard.

Until all my fears drain away, and all I'm left with

is a promise of more.
    And hopefully, one day, her love in return.

EPILOGUE

KASSIDY
Two Months Later

"What can I get for you, handsome?"

It's almost closing time at Maximum when Jarett walks in. Monday nights are the quietest evening shift of the week, and Max prefers me to close while she catches up on administrative tasks.

"Depends, beautiful. What are you offering?" He grins widely and winks as he pulls up a stool at the bar.

Over the past month or so, Jarett has stuck to his promise of staying out of my work life, including my casual work at the speakeasy and my assignment with Lugreno.

Jarett's work, on the other hand, I have very much become a part of. Lazing around his apartment in the nude is all the inspiration he needs to set up his easel and paint. His joy when creating art is permeable, and the accomplishment once a new canvas is complete makes every moment worth being his muse.

Setting his whiskey on the bar, I lean over and plant a kiss on his lips. Yeah, he still takes it upon himself to meet me here for a drink while I close up and see that I get home safely, but I'm not complaining about my guy being a gentleman.

Since my return from Australia, Jarett and I have settled into a comfortable routine.

"We staying at your place or mine tonight, love?" he asks over his glass.

"Yours, I'm out of coffee." I chuckle. We only spend a few nights together each week now as opposed to every night. We both agree on taking things slow because so much has changed for each of us in a short amount of time.

"I might have to buy shares in coffee pods, love. I've never known anyone to consume coffee the way you do." He laughs, shaking his head.

Throwing him a smile over my shoulder as I finish wiping down the bar, I know there's nothing he won't do for me. Once I let go of the fear and false belief that I can only have a career *or* a man in my life, my days are blessed with happiness, friendship, and laughter again.

And love.

I am unequivocally in love with Jarett Evans,

secret billionaire and art extraordinaire. He is my person, and I refuse to consider what my life will look like as I near the end of my contract with Lugreno. I choose to believe fate has us covered, and we'll get through any obstacles together.

Half an hour later, I'm locking up, and Jarett helps drag me up the stairs. I recently started back at the gym, and my spin instructor is an evil bitch. My legs are so tight, I wince with each step I take, but I won't miss a class for anything. Besides needing to work through the pain, I have come to enjoy seeing a special group of ladies regularly.

Life in London is made for me. The summer nights are beautiful, a vast contrast to when I first arrived. I especially love that we commute most places on foot or a short trip on the subway where necessary.

"Let's get you home and into bed, love." Jarett laughs at my pained grin and wraps his arms around my shoulders.

JARETT

"I was starting to think you weren't going to make it," Sophia greets us both with a peck on the cheek. Stunning as always in her evening gown and perfectly styled updo, I'm positive she lives for these gala events. Me, I can do without them, but she's a warrior at heart, and I will always support her.

"Wouldn't have missed it for the world," I tell her and shake Roman's hand once he's finished greeting my woman.

Kassidy and Sophia exchange pleasantries and compliments as I chat with Roman and scope out the ballroom. For years now, Sophia has been a huge advocate of human trafficking, and she runs an annual charity auction to raise funds for the foundation she personally funded.

A waitress swings past and offers a flute of bubbly. "Thank you," Kassidy swoons, taking a glass for her and Sophia while Roman and I both glance over at the bar.

"Why don't we go get us some real drinks, bro?"

Nodding, Roman starts on his way before I can let go of Kassidy's hand.

"A few whiskeys to get us through the auction, and we can escape before the dancing begins, yeah?"

I glance over at him as we brush through the crowd. "Unfortunately for me, I think Kassidy will want to stay and support our sister through to the end."

Roman chuckles. "Pussy-whipped fucker."

As we approach the ladies with our tumblers of whiskey, I spot Gabe Lugreno. "The fuck is he doing here?"

"I never did get much detail from Sophia as to how he ended up as her date for her birthday. Did you?" Roman's question reminds me of the night which could have ruined everything for Kassidy and me.

"No, I had more pressing matters to deal with following that night."

Kassidy is speaking with Gabe as we join them. "I didn't realize you were in town. Are we set to start on the contract?"

Gabe's eyes flicker to mine, and I nod in acknowledgment, lacing my arm around Kassidy's waist. Sophia appears nervous and avoids eye contact with any of us as if she's busy searching the room for somebody of importance or a valid reason to escape the conversation.

"Ah no, this trip is all pleasure." Gabe grins and nestles closer to Sophia, his arm around her back, hand positioned protectively on her hip. "We met at this event last year, your sister and I. Seems we have many things in common."

Seeing my sister with a date is unusual at best. For a woman who spends her life creating perfect matches and setting up dates that often lead to weddings and more, she's not one for relationships of her own. At least not publicly. But when she smiles up at Gabe, her emotion surprises me. I knock back a sip of whiskey, my gaze narrowing in on the multi-billionaire and his perfect hair, who has an undeniable attraction to my sister. I missed all of this at her birthday.

Clearing my throat, I do my best to remain neutral. "So, you two have been dating for a whole year?" The fact I am in business with this guy, and he's been banging my sister for fuck knows how long, grates on my nerves.

"Yes," Gabe answers at the same time Sophia says, "No."

"Okay, well, this has been lovely. When do the auctions begin, Sophia?" Kassidy chimes in with a change of subject and pinches my ass. I stare down at her tucked into my shoulder, and she returns my gaze with a pointed look.

Not now.

"Yes, I should get a move on. This event won't run itself. Thank you all for being here." She smiles, and I'm left wondering what the fuck when she pulls Gabe in for a heated kiss. Seconds later, she floats toward the stage while the four of us are left staring at each other.

"I trust this won't be awkward for you, Jarett, with us being in business together. Or for you Kassidy," Gabe turns in her direction.

"You mean the fact you're fucking my sister?" The words fall from my lips louder than expected, bringing his attention back to me.

A pointed smirk pulls at his lips. "Expect to be seeing a lot more of me."

Kassidy takes the bait immediately. "Oh, is the timeline moving up on our project?"

He shakes his head back and forth slowly, his eyes never leave mine. "No, this is strictly personal."

"Sophia's not the dating type, so whatever you're thinking, don't."

Gabe chuckles as he lifts his glass to his lips and Kassidy places her hand in mine. A subtle reminder to keep myself in check.

"I meet a lot of women on my travels, but none who have affected me like Sophia. She may not realize it yet, but we're meant to be together."

Roman and I roar with laughter and Kassidy tenses beside me.

Gabe remains silent, his glare thick with dislike.

"Mark my words... I'll do whatever it takes to make her mine."

The End

Next in the series:
My Billionaire Fling: Gabe and Sophia's Story
(British Billionaires Book 2)

My Five Night Fling

Other Series by Maci Dillon

British Billionaires

Unrequited Love

Twice the Fun

Beachmont Players

And more…

Subscribe to the Minx Diaries
and receive a FREE eBook.
https://macidillonauthor.com/subscribe

Join Maci Dillon's Reader Group
https://facebook.com/groups/macidillonminxes

ACKNOWLEDGMENTS

Bossman, thank you for putting up with my crazy through yet another book. The past few months have been a wild and trying ride. Your patience, support, and extra pampering mean the word to me. I love you. xx

My beautiful girls, I know my writing takes away from our time together sometimes, but I promise, in the years to come, it will all be worth it. Your laughter, love, and constant encouragement keep me going every day. xx

Sara, my fabulous PA. Fuck, I would be lost without you. Thank you for everything you do, and damn, I know it's a lot of work. You rock. xx

Minxes, bring on the margaritas, my treat! Your ongoing support, encouragement, friendship, and messages are the best! Without you, I'd be a lonely writer in a straitjacket. Thank you. xx

Kaylene and Nicki at Swish, you make this process so seamless. You're both a blast to work with. I can't thank you both enough. And of course, Kim for the graphics too – I love them! Thank you. xx

Sarah Paige at Opium, I love the covers for this series even better than the first, which I didn't think was possible. It is an absolute pleasure working with you. Thank you. xx

Special mention to my beta readers, Ellen, Belinda, and Carol – this book was a mess when you got it. Thank you for your honest feedback and suggestions, which made this book what it is. xx

To my ARC tribe, bloggers, book influencers, readers, and reviewers. Without you all, this book would never have seen the light of day. I appreciate your time taken to read this series, provide honest feedback and reviews, and share with your reader friends and followers. I can never thank you enough. From the bottom of my heart, thank you. xx

Best wishes,
Maci Dillon

ABOUT THE Author

Maci Dillon is a self-confessed lover of margaritas who has recently experienced her very own second chance at true romance.

Maci is a daydreamer and true minx at heart who loves to read and write steamy romance filled with love, lust, angst, and humor. Her favorite tropes to write are second chances, forbidden romance, enemies to lovers, menage, reverse harem, hate sex, drunken hookups, playboys, and billionaires. She also enjoys writing raunchy short stories within these tropes.

Her heroines are strong, experienced, foul-mouthed, and feisty with loads of sass and wit. Her men are deliciously hot, dominant, often arrogant, and entitled smart-asses. You will experience all the feels across Maci's books.

You will often find Maci in her PJs writing and watching Netflix. She is an expert procrastinator, a superior planner, except with her writing, and loves a social drink and barbecue with friends and family.

Maci lives in Brisbane, Australia, and is a mother of three teenagers and a Maltese Shih Tzu.

Visit my Website!
https://macidillonauthor.com/

Printed in Great Britain
by Amazon